OOPS-A-DAISY

THE DE LA CRUZ DIARIES

MELODY DELGADO

Clean Reads
GREAT STORIES. NO GUILT.
www.cleanreads.com

Oops-a-Daisy
by Melody Delgado
Published by Clean Reads
www.cleanreads.com

OOPS-A-DAISY
Copyright © 2017 MELODY DELGADO
ISBN 978-1-62135-699-8
Cover Art Designed by CORA GRAPHICS

For Chuck, Sarah and Jonathan

ACKNOWLEDGMENTS

Many eyes saw drafts of this story, and it wouldn't have moved on to completion without the help of other writers, editors and friends, so many thanks go to the following people:

Lou F. read the first draft and provided honest and helpful insights.

My local SCBWI group members, Kelly, Janet, June and Robin helped keep me on track and digging deeper.

Rhonda T. and Cassidy T. double-checked my musical references.

J.R. and Evelyn F. and Luz helped to make sure my Spanish words and phrases were accurate.

Kelly G. reviewed and helped me cut down my final draft.

My editors, Stephanie, Julie, Victoria and Janet, helped improve and polish the manuscript.

Verla K. and all the administrators, moderators, and members, past and present, of the SCBWI Blueboards who have given helpful advice over the years.

Special thanks to Betty G. for sharing all the shenanigans and also to my agent, Cyle Young, for his work on Daisy's behalf.

And last, but certainly not least, thanks to God for blessing me by allowing me to come in contact with the people mentioned above.

PUERQUITO THE PASTA LOVER

Okay, so I was standing in the middle of a television studio about to shoot my first commercial. *Woohoo!* I'd been dreaming of getting my big break for a super long time. Like three whole weeks to be exact. All right, so maybe I'd been waiting my whole life. Well, not exactly my whole life, but for at least two years I'd dreamed of nothing else but becoming the next Gloria Florez. And since G-Flo started out in commercials, I figured I was on the right track.

"Places!" a stagehand hollered.

I bolted to the set, which was designed to look like an average kitchen.

"You Daisy De La Cruz?" the stagehand asked me.

"Oh...um...yeah...I mean yes!"

He pointed to a piece of masking tape stuck to the floor. "If you'll come over here and stand on your mark, we're just about ready to shoot."

I rushed over to the spot as quickly as I could, considering I was wearing a shaggy dog costume with about twenty tons of fake fur hanging from it, and slid a rubber doggy mask over my sweaty head. My long brown hair had been blown dried that morning so it would be sleek and straight, but with all the heat and humidity it was starting to curl and frizz. But, hey, I finally had my first shot at show business, so I wasn't about to complain.

Once I was in position, a Miss America look-alike wearing too much make-up joined me on the set.

"Lights! Camera! Take one!" *Snap.*

Miss America gazed into the camera and sang to the tune of *London Bridge.*

Queeny once had stinky breath,
stinky breath, stinky breath.
Yuck! I almost choked to death.
Now she's better.

I came in on cue, continuing the song.

Mom gave me some Stink-Away,
Stink-Away, Stink-Away.
Now my breath is A-Okay,
I'm all better.
Aooooooo!

The announcer's voice piped in. "*Stink-Away* is all natural and safe. Side effects may include loud barking, non-stop scratching, and increased car chasing. Why not try *Stink-Away* today?"

"Cut!" the director hollered. "Let's try it again. This time, Queeny, howl like you mean it."

By the time we ran through sixteen takes, I was dripping so much sweat that my howl was full of meaning.

The director fingered his beard and exhaled loudly. "Why don't we take a short break?"

As I wrenched off my mask and searched for a place to sit, I realized my dark hair was so sweaty it was totally matted to my head. There was a bench outside, so I headed toward the exit, but once I realized there'd be no chance for a breeze, I decided to stay inside. The only thing waiting for me out there was a giant dose of Miami summer steam.

After trudging down the hall a few more steps, some furniture came into view. I dropped onto a leather couch so hard and fast it groaned. I leaned back and pulled a piece of paper from a hollow ear inside the mask. It was a letter from my grandfather. To me, my grandfather was just about perfect. He was one of my favorite people because he always managed to see the good in things and had a way of making me laugh no matter what was happening.

And he didn't think my dreams were stupid or a waste of time, either. Some of my other relatives rolled their eyes whenever I talked about my plans, but not him. He'd never even think about not supporting me.

We didn't get to see each other often, though, because he didn't exactly live close by. Since my *Abuelo* lived in Puerto Rico, he spoke fluent Spanish, but he was still trying to learn English. I'd already scanned his note five or six times that day even though it was a little tricky to understand, but I unfolded it and read it again.

To a speshel grill,

I hapy you making crumercial. Now you on your way to bee big star. I no you will go farm and become a big celery. I wish I could have tocked longer on the fon the udder day but it was getting late and it was time to eat my zipper. I look forward to visit you soon.

P.S. Hapy 12 birdday – Use the chick to by what you want two.

Lov,

Your favorit Grandfeather

"LET'S ROLL!" THE STAGEHAND HOLLERED.

So much for rest and relaxation. When I'm heading up my own studio the actors won't get a measly little five-minute break. No way! I'll give them at least six.

I hurried back to the set and stood in position. We ran through the entire commercial again and did it exactly like every other take we'd done. I crossed my fingers and waited.

"Cut!" the director hollered. "That's a wrap."

Phew! I felt as wet as if I'd been surfing at Miami Beach, but that was a small sacrifice to make for my first paying gig. *Woohoo!* I couldn't believe I was getting paid just for dressing up and singing. I'd have to be sure to thank my agent for helping me get the gig.

Miss America hit me with a high-five before batting her false eyelashes at the director. "Ya'll got any more shoots coming up? For something like jewelry or perfume?" She glanced over at me then whispered, "For humans?" What did she think? I was a real dog and I'd be insulted if I overheard? Either she was a nickel short of a dollar in the brains department or my acting was incredibly convincing.

"Let's see." The director scanned a chart on the wall. "Warts, cold sores, athlete's foot fungus...Any of those interest you?"

"Of course!" Miss America's eyelashes fluttered again. "Give me a ring. Toodles." She smiled, waved, and strode out as if she had just won another pageant.

Maybe he's got another commercial for me, too. Something that'll get me some attention. "You shooting anything that'll air like...nationally?"

The director eyed my doggie getup and laughed. "Not at the moment, Queeny. But I'll be sure to call your agent if I need a singing cat."

"Great! I meow much better than I can howl."

He laughed again and took off in a hurry.

My shoulders started to slouch, but I quickly straightened

them. *G-Flo's first commercial was for kitty litter and now she's topping the charts with her music and movies. When you start at the bottom the only place to go is up, right?*

I rounded the corner casually then ripped off my mask and trotted toward the water cooler, feeling a sudden urge to lap up the water with my tongue. I guzzled what seemed like gallons of cool, clear liquid before my mother found me, helped me change back into normal clothes, and led me outside to her shiny, new, fuel-efficient hybrid.

Once we got home, I rushed upstairs to shower. As I dried myself off in my bedroom, I thought about calling Miss Palmer, my music teacher at the Rosenthal School of the Arts. Miss Palmer was the one who suggested I look for an agent. She might want to know that her advice had helped me get results. But I decided not to bug her over summer vacation. We could talk about the shoot when school started in a couple of weeks.

The phone rang as I pulled a T-shirt over my head. It was my best friend, Tamika. I was hoping she was calling to invite me to the beach. My dad only took us in the evenings, so we wouldn't get sunburns. Tamika's family went whenever they felt like it, as in normal daytime hours.

"You won't believe this," she said in a rush.

I sprawled out on my unmade bed. Tamika was a talker, and something like getting a new toothbrush could excite her. "Let me guess? You went to the dentist, and he gave you a sticker for being good?"

"Miss Palmer won't be back next year."

I shot into an upright position. "What?"

"I just heard. The PTA meeting is still going on in the living room. Everyone was talking about it when I went to the kitchen for a drink."

"You must've heard wrong." I stood up. "She would have told me!"

"She had to rush off to help her sick mother in New York."

I gripped the phone tighter. "That means she won't be here on the first day of school. We won't even get a chance to say goodbye."

"Yeah, it totally stinks. But get this. They've already found someone to take her place."

"No way!"

"A Scottish professor is moving here from some conservatory in London. Wait till you hear his name. Professor Romeo Nigel Magoon. Does he sound like a total loser or what?" Tamika's voice dropped to a whisper. "Gotta run. My dad's headed this way, and I'm not supposed to know anything."

I felt like I'd fallen so hard the wind was knocked out of me. Miss Palmer had been my teacher since first grade. We'd gotten close after being together for five years. I trusted her so much she almost felt like an aunt, or an older sister. It wasn't like she was just teaching me and helping me. She believed in me and seemed to think I had a shot at fulfilling my dreams. I sat on my bed trying to let the news sink in.

After a few minutes, I threw on some shorts and headed downstairs to look for my mother. She was in the kitchen stirring a pot of black beans. I sat on a stool and picked at the cotton stuffing erupting from a hole in the cushion. "Miss Palmer's gone. She won't be coming back next year."

Mom pushed her short, straight hair behind her ears and gave me a hug. "Oh no. I'm so sorry, *mija*. Miss Palmer believed in you. What happened?"

I took a deep breath and filled her in on what Tamika told me. Mom measured rice into a pot that was so old and black it looked like a cauldron.

"Miss Palmer was a real gem, but you might learn a lot from her replacement, too. Who knows? He might have connections with other artist types and even be able to help Rosa."

Just then, my five-year-old sister popped out from hiding in the pantry. "I'm gonna sing like Daisy. I'm gonna sing like Daisy," Rosa chanted. Her brown curls bounced as she daintily held the hem of her floral-print dress and skipped from the room.

While Mom finished cooking dinner, I rested my chin in my hands and thought about the good times I'd had with Miss Palmer and all she'd taught me. It would be tough adjusting to a new teacher. But Mom was right. There were still a lot of things I wanted to learn. I needed to give the new guy a chance and work hard to show him I was a serious student.

Dad wandered into the kitchen with sage green paint splattered all over his ripped jeans and sneakers. "One bathroom down, the entire house to go. So much for buying a big, old fixer-upper." He wrenched off his baseball cap, wiped his balding head with a paper towel and scrubbed his hands under the sink. "Sorry it's taken so long to get started."

Long? Try two years, Papasito.

"I'll get to your rooms next, girls. I promise," Dad said.

I wondered if my grandfather's upcoming visit had anything to do with Dad's sudden urge to spruce things up. As if a coat of paint was the only thing our ancient house needed.

Rosa scurried in from the living room shouting, "Pink, pink, pink! I want pink!"

"Hmm," I said. "I'm not so sure I want pink in my room."

"Fine." Dad grabbed a spoon and snatched a bite of rice. "I'll paint Rosa's room first. Rosa, why don't you come with me when I pick out the color?"

"Okay." She gazed up at him with her huge brown eyes. "After we pick out the dog you promised."

I smirked. "You only get a dog if you quit complaining about starting school."

"Ah, *sí*." Dad nodded. "I forgot about the dog."

Rosa hopped up and down. "You can't forget! I can't wait to

start kindergarten. It's my most favoritist thing in the world. Kindergarten rocks!"

Dad dried his hands. "Something tells me I'll have someone to remind me."

———

AFTER DAD BROUGHT MOM AND ME HOME AFTER CHURCH, HE took Rosa to the pound to pick out a dog, as promised.

Rosa raced into the house an hour later. "See my new doggie!" She carried what looked like a filthy mop.

"What is that?" I asked, backing away from her. I didn't see any eyes, a nose, or a mouth, just a mass of dirty, gray hair. "It looks creepy."

"I know." Rosa put the dog down and clapped her hands. "That's why I picked it!"

———

AFTER ROSA AND DAD GAVE THE DOG A BATH, IT WENT FROM looking like a mop to resembling a swatch of white carpet. A neighbor told them it was a living, breathing life form known as a Maltese. And could that thing eat. It must have been half-starved. Only a high-voltage vacuum cleaner could suck up food faster.

A walking piece of carpet with a vacuum for a mouth described him perfectly. And he looked just like the costume I wore in the *Stink-Away* commercial. I only had to look at him to be reminded of sweating like a pig. And his breath! He was the perfect candidate for a free *Stink-Away* sample. That was it, I decided. *Puerquito.* Little pig would be his name. It suited him perfectly. I just had to convince Rosa.

"Here, Puerquito," I called.

"Oh! I like that name!" Rosa cried. "You're my little pig, aren't you?" She scooped him up and kissed him till he growled at her.

———

ON THE FIRST DAY OF SCHOOL, PUERQUITO ACTED JUST LIKE HIS namesake. I poured Rosa a bowl of cereal and as soon as she wandered off to find a spoon, he hopped from a kitchen chair to the table and devoured her breakfast. I poured her a new bowl, and he wolfed it down again. We couldn't get rid of him until I wrenched open the door leading to the back yard. Talk about a little pig! *Yes, Puerquito is the perfect name for him, unless we call him Hairy-Alien-Trash-Eating-Stinky-Breath-Puff-Ball.*

Dad drove us to school a few minutes later. It was only a short ride to my arts magnet school, which was just like a regular elementary school, but with a focus on the arts.

As we meandered down winding lanes and passed rows of older homes, I started squirming like a toddler. It was hard to know what to expect from Professor Magoon with all the rumors flying around. The name Romeo *did* have an elegant ring to it. *Maybe he'll end up being as handsome as his name. He could turn out to be a nice guy after all and be able to help me just as much as Miss Palmer did.* I knew I had to meet him and make a good impression as soon as possible.

When I got to class, all Mrs. Sandberg had us do was set up our desks. Since we weren't busy, I thought about ways of sneaking out to meet Professor Magoon. *I can pretend to sprain my ankle. But that will only bring me as far as the nurse's office – with someone helping.*

I tried to concentrate when Mrs. Sandberg finally gave us a reading assignment, but my thoughts kept getting interrupted by visions of the professor's handsome face.

When the lunch bell finally rang, I reached for my wallet,

but it was empty. Instead of sneaking off to the music room to catch a glimpse of my new teacher, I found myself in the school office calling home.

"Hello, Dad?" I said into the phone beside the secretary's desk. "I forgot my lunch money. Can you bail me out?"

"Your timing is perfect," said Dad, out of breath. "I'm about to take Puerquito to the vet. I'll be right there."

"Great."

"Oh, and one more thing."

I shifted the phone to my other ear. "What?"

"I wanted to tell you to quit chewing the carpet you little non-stop-eating-machine! Get outside you creepy... shaggy... thingy!" There was loud barking then a door slammed shut.

"Dad?"

"Sorry," he said. "I just wanted to tell you to stop that yapping I can't even hear myself think!"

I tapped my fingers on the wooden counter. "Dad my lunch break is only—"

"Sorry. I wanted to tell you I'll be painting your room next, so think about what color you want."

I trudged outdoors to wait on the concrete steps beside the carpool drop-off. As I watched for approaching cars, I imagined my first meeting with my new music teacher. *I'll be extra polite and use my best manners, so he'll be able to recognize me as the star I'm destined to become. I'll bring him his morning coffee, help him conduct the choir, work with him on important musical productions...*

The sound of a bird rustling in a nearby palm tree startled me. As I breathed in, smelling a mixture of bug repellant and fertilizer, an ancient convertible with the top down, screeched to a halt in front of the curb.

"Sorry to keep you waiting," Dad said breathlessly. "The people at the pound didn't give me a leash when I picked him up yesterday. I had a hard time getting him in the car." He tossed me the money. "Here's your *dinero*. I've got to hurry to make my appointment."

I leaned against the dusty car. "Whoa! Dad, wait a minute!"

"*¿Qué pasa?*"

I frowned. "Your clothes are covered in paint. Your hair and eyebrows are pink. I can't believe you left the house looking like this."

Dad sighed. "It was either get cleaned up or leave you to starve."

"Okay, *Papi*. It's just that—"

Puerquito seized the opportunity to jump from the back seat of the motionless car and hit the pavement running.

I chased him, but all my short arms managed to grab was hot air, not Puerquito. He blew past me, scurrying inside the brick building in between the black jazz shoes of some dance instructors who were leaving.

Dad hollered from the car. "I'll park. Go in after him. Don't lose him!"

Sprinting up the concrete steps, I spotted the fur ball bounding across the beige tiled floor and heading toward the cafeteria and the strong odor of burnt spaghetti sauce. I followed, rushed into the lunchroom, and spotted the little pig causing a big commotion at the sixth-grade tables.

All the kids in my class stared as Puerquito landed on their table and plodded over plates of spaghetti. He snarfed bites of pasta as he worked his way down his own personal buffet. His creamy white fur was soon covered in red sauce.

Some of the kids cheered as they stood up and watched from behind their chairs.

"Wow!"

"Go, dog!"

"Do it again!"

After knocking over several cartons of open milk, Puerquito

eyed a huge juicy meatball a few plates down. He rushed over to it, sniffed it, licked it, and swallowed it whole in one gulp. Then he started coughing and hacking. As he gave one mighty belch, the meatball hurtled out of his mouth and landed on the other end of the table. He ran back to it, sniffed it, licked it, and swallowed it whole again.

Tamika yelled, "How gross!"

I witnessed it all from the next table, where I stood frozen. *I have to be watching a video of someone else's life. This embarrassing moment can't possibly be a scene from mine.*

A pudgy man with graying hair sticking out in every direction bustled over from the other side of the large, noise-filled cafeteria.

"What in the world is going on here?" he asked, glaring at Puerquito.

At that moment, Dad rushed in. Surveying the damage, he quickly scooped up Puerquito before he could attack another plate of spaghetti. "I can splain," Dad said to the man. Dad's accent always got stronger when he was nervous.

The midget of a man stared up at Dad through thick, horn-rimmed glasses. "Who are you?"

Dad stared at the tomato-splattered floor, mumbling, "*Yo soy*...I mean...I'm Dr. Juan Ramon De La Cruz. The, uh, father of one of the students here."

I wandered over to my father and whispered, "Dad, don't you think you and Puerquito should leave now?"

"Ah, *sí*. Jes. I mean yes. Again, I'm so sorry," he said. "I'm buying him a leash today. This will never happen again."

As Dad made to leave, Puerquito shook himself off. Large drops of sauce landed all over my white blouse, as well as the glasses of Mr. Stubby-Little-Elf.

He wiped the sauce off his glasses with a scowl. "See that it doesn't." My father made his escape. The man took a deep breath, shook his head and glanced back toward the kids in my class. "I suggest those of you in need of a new lunch get back in line immediately."

Cinnamon Cleaver threw her huge mass of rust-colored waves over her shoulder and stomped her foot. "We'll be late for modern dance." Her thin figure and up-to-the-minute clothes gave her the look of a young supermodel, except for her nose, which was slightly too big for her face.

She'd landed the lead in almost every school play until I managed to snatch the lead from her last spring. And she'd held a grudge against me ever since.

The man flapped his arms like a goose collecting its goslings. "Dance class can wait. Let's keep things moving. At this rate, we'll have to ask for tomorrow's breakfast menu."

Cinnamon turned around in line, shooting me with invisible I-so-do-not-like-you x-ray beams. "What do you have to say for yourself, now?"

"Oops-a-daisy?" said Tamika's twin brother, Brad. His dreadlocks shook against his baggy T-shirt, so it was obvious he was trying not to laugh.

"Enough with the chatter, Mr. Robinson," said the man.

Brad's grin disappeared as he hung his head. "Sorry, Professor."

The air slowly drained from my lungs. I gripped the back of a chair for support. "W-what did you call him?" *Please, please, please. There's no way he can possibly be—*

"Young lady." The man stood tall, raising his chin as if on stage, ready to burst into song. "My name is Professor Magoon. Professor Romeo Nigel Magoon."

QUEEN OF THE SCHOOL

"May I p-please go to the girl's room to clean up my b-blouse?"

Professor Magoon eyed me like I had a contagious disease. "Yes, please do."

I did not just make my first impression on this guy in the cafeteria of all places. And that creepy little spaghetti monster of a dog did not introduce us. No way!

I entered the tiled bathroom, bent over a sink, and splashed my hot face with cool water.

The door opened behind me. "You okay?" It was Tamika. After I dried myself off I saw the look of concern on her face. It was nice of her to offer support.

I took a deep breath. "Do you think what just happened was a total and complete disaster or a minor disaster? Because a total and complete disaster is not something I can handle right now."

Tamika crossed her arms and made a face. "It was definitely a disaster. But on a scale of one to ten, I'd give it a three. That would make it a teeny-tiny disaster."

I leaned against a white porcelain sink. "Good. I can live with that."

Tamika pulled a pick from her jeans and fluffed her inch-long Afro. "Puerquito is one cute little puppy, even if he is a total mess. But I hear you. I don't want to get on Professor Magoon's bad side, either."

"What else have you heard?" I dabbed at my blouse with a wet paper towel.

The door banged open and in sauntered Cinnamon Cleaver with her jewelry jangling and her high heels *click-click-clicking* across the floor. Cinnamon let the door slam behind her and marched right up to me. "If you wanted Magoon to notice you, Miss Attention-Seeker, he did."

"Hello! If I wanted him to notice me, don't you think I would've come up with a better way to get his attention?" I dabbed at my blouse with another towel, trying to dry it.

Cinnamon scowled. Her face became almost as red as her frilly, expensive blouse. "Whatever! Your disgusting mutt got sauce all over my white designer sandals. They're, like, a couple hundred dollars, not that you'd know."

"White is sooo not practical," I mumbled, tossing my paper towel in the trash and ignoring the fact that I wore white myself.

Tamika giggled.

"What was that?" Cinnamon snapped.

"I'm sorry about your sandals," I said. "But he's not my dog, he's—"

"Adorable," Tamika cut in.

"Whatever!" Cinnamon ripped her shoes off and rinsed them under the sink. "I should make you pay for these, but you probably can't afford designer prices. I'll be stuck dying them red."

I blew on my blouse hoping it would dry faster. "How do you know what I can afford? I earned some money over the summer."

Cinnamon put her sandals back on. "Like we need to be

reminded that you landed your first commercial. Ooooh! Goodie goodie for you."

"You can get an agent and audition for stuff, too, you know."

"Believe me, now that my mom's back in town, I'm going to," Cinnamon said, storming off.

"That girl is one snootie-patootie!" Tamika said, shaking her head.

"I've heard that can happen when you always get what you want."

"Not anymore." Tamika smirked. "Not with you suddenly pulling up from behind."

Yeah, I pull up from behind and look what happens. Some people hate me. Others get jealous. I was done wasting my energy thinking about someone as spoiled rotten as Cinnamon Cleaver. I headed for the door. "So much for trying to eat lunch."

"I got a few bites down before your dog trashed my plate," said Tamika. "Let's go see if we've got time to make it through the line."

Tiny green lizards scrambled in and out of palmetto bushes and onto the sidewalk as we rushed back to the cafeteria. I spotted a poster on the wall and stopped to read it.

THE ROSENTHAL SCHOOL OF THE ARTS PRESENTS:

LA ISLA DEL ENCANTO – A MUSICAL EXTRAVAGANZA

All students in kindergarten through sixth-grade welcome to audition

"A musical about Puerto Rico? No way," I said. "That's where my parents are from."

"It's supposed to be a big deal," Tamika said. "It might be a great chance to get discovered."

"Discovered? By who?"

Tamika's hands moved around wildly. They did that whenever she got excited. "That's what I was trying to tell you a minute ago. Big Bad Magoon is asking all kinds of big wigs to come and see the show."

"Where'd you hear that?" I asked her.

"My mom's PTA President, remember?" Tamika was smiling so wide and showing so many teeth she reminded me of the cat from *Alice in Wonderland*. "She's got a big mouth, and I've got big ears."

I wondered if what Tamika said was true. It was hard to know for sure because she exaggerated sometimes. She wouldn't do it on purpose, or anything. But she just got excited about little things super easily and then made them out to be bigger than what they actually were.

Like last year during winter break. She called me up and said she had a paying gig for both of us. And we'd be singing in front of lots of people. So I got all dressed up. She and her mother drove over to pick me up and we ended up pulling into the parking lot of some fancy-pants building that looked like an old-time plantation.

"Where are we?" I asked.

"Macon Manor. It's a nursing home," Mrs. Robinson said. "My grandmother lives here. Our church choir comes over every Christmas Eve to sing for the residents."

We wandered inside, and Tamika sang her little heart out. She had two solos, but she let me sing a few lines of *Jingle Bells.* They passed around a basket afterwards, and a bunch of seniors tossed their spare change into it. The choir let Tamika and me split the loot. We each made a whopping $2.73. *Woohoo!*

Since Tamika hadn't sung many solos in public before, it was a big deal for her. But I didn't mind going along with Tamika when she made a big deal out of things because being easy to please made her fun to be around.

I turned away from the poster and started hustling toward the lunchroom again.

"I sure hope they have more meatballs," Tamika said, following.

"Me too," I said as my stomach let out a huge growl.

But as soon as we plowed through the cafeteria doors, the bell rang, signaling the end of lunch.

———

I got a shock later that afternoon when Mrs. Sandberg told us to line up for music. I was sooo not ready to see the professor again. One of the things my mother had loved about Miss Palmer was her nurturing personality. I didn't understand what that meant at first, but I think what she meant was that Miss Palmer had been approachable and kind. Which made it easy for us not to worry so much about making mistakes, or forgetting our lines, or whatever. Miss Palmer had just wanted us to do our best. Being perfect wasn't something she expected.

Something told me the professor was playing by a different set of rules. And it didn't seem like being nurturing was going to be his strong point.

When we entered the music room I grabbed hold of Tamika's arm as I climbed the risers. Her brother, Brad, followed us. He must have sensed we needed extra support, since Brad was good at noticing things. We found seats on the top riser because I wanted to hide behind the other kids. Maybe, this way, the professor would forget who I was. Then next time we met, I'd be starting off with a clean slate.

Professor Magoon stepped out of his office looking as confident as a model gliding on a catwalk. He took a seat in a fancy upholstered chair that looked like it belonged in a fancy living room. "I thought I'd start by filling you in on a few details about myself. As most of you know, my name is Professor Romeo Nigel Magoon."

Giggles erupted around the room as he said his first name. He nodded, nonplussed.

"Ah, yes, the joy of being named after a Shakespearean character." Even though he was on the short side and we sat above him on the risers, it felt like he was towering over us. "While I was born in Scotland, most of my musical training was done in London."

"Can you play the bagpipes?" a boy named Enrique asked.

Professor Magoon's eyebrows shot up. "I have been called an old windbag. Does that count?"

Giggles erupted again.

He seems to have a sense of humor. Maybe he won't be so bad.

"My signature role was that of Tamino in Mozart's magnificent opera, *The Magic Flute...*" The professor droned on and on, slowly pacing the room, dropping names of people he had performed with, most of whom I had never heard of but who were probably important in the world of classical music.

Talk about connections, this guy sounds like he knows every musician on the planet.

He stopped pacing. "I'm sure many of you have seen the posters I've placed around the school concerning our upcoming musical. I understand that in the past, the singers and dancers were not separated. But you've come to an age when it will be best to specialize and find your niche, at least for now. There are only so many performers who can do everything well. So, there will be lead singing roles as well as parts for lead dancers."

Phew! That takes Cinnamon out of the way since she'll probably try out for lead dancer. She's sure to get it. Then maybe she'll finally leave me alone.

"I'm also making plans for a master class that will feature intensive training from myself, as well as a select group of industry professionals."

Professionals? From where?

Tamika nudged me, but I kept looking straight ahead. I didn't want to miss a word the professor was saying.

"I wish I could offer everyone the chance to participate in this advanced class, but as the training will be hands on, only twelve sixth graders will be invited to participate. These twelve spots will be reserved for those who prove themselves serious about learning, supporting, and performing in the arts."

Cinnamon raised her hand. "Will landing a solo in the musical help?"

The professor nodded. "Indeed. Those desiring to be in the

master class should take the upcoming audition seriously. If you prepare well and procure a solo, while you're not guaranteed a spot, you'll likely obtain one."

There it is. I've got to land the lead singing role in the musical.

Brad glanced at me and raised his hand. "What if someone does professional work outside of school, but doesn't get a solo, will they qualify?"

"Certainly. Anyone serious about their training will qualify for the master class."

A kid named Enrique raised his hand. "When will we know who makes it?"

"Good question." Professor Magoon began pacing again. "The selection process will be done after the performance, as the master class will begin shortly thereafter." The professor stroked his chin. "Try outs for the musical will be held three weeks from today. Out of curiosity, how many of you think you have the courage to follow in my footsteps by auditioning for a part?"

Almost every hand went up. Cinnamon flipped her red hair over her shoulders and stuck her nose in the air. *She knows she's a shoe-in for lead dancer. Fine with me.*

"Is there a good time to come by your office to ask for audition advice?" I blurted out before I could stop myself. Miss Palmer always helped us with our song choices.

Professor Magoon glared at me like I was a hair he'd just found in his soup. Talk about disgusted. "Good heavens, don't tell me you're used to being spoon fed! Finding audition material is *your* responsibility. I will supply the audition location, which will be here, and the sound system, which is there," he said pointing to the brand new, state-of-the-art equipment.

Wow. Things are definitely going to be different around here. How in the world am I ever supposed to win this guy over?

"Why do only twelve kids get to be in the master class?" a girl named Emma asked. "Why can't everyone be in it?"

The professor frowned. "My dear, for every one of *you* there are hundreds of others desiring what you want. Aspiring to the arts is a brutal business. In order to make it, you must not only be the most talented, but you must also be the toughest, hardest working, and most determined. You will learn this lesson and you will learn it now. Otherwise, feel free to attend a traditional school and learn how to add."

He is one tough cookie.

The bell rang. "Your homework assignment is on the board. More about the musical next time." The professor bowed and retreated to his office as murmurs erupted around the room.

It seemed like everyone was sizing up everyone else, trying to figure out who was going to make it into the master class. There were twenty-four sixth graders in our class and twenty-four in Mrs. Blake's. That meant everyone had a one in four chance of making it.

There were lots of talented kids in both classes, so the spots were totally up for grabs. All I knew was I had to get to work on my song right away if I was going to snatch a vocal solo.

Cinnamon was the only person who was guaranteed to grab a spot. But that didn't seem to matter. She seemed ready to pounce as she scanned the room, whispering to her cronies, who plastered me with dirty looks. She had to know there was no way I'd even think about competing with her for lead dancer.

So much for hoping she'd forgive and forget. I had the nerve to try and dethrone her from her position as the one and only Queen of the School, and I was going to pay for it. Forever.

LA ISLA DEL ENCANTO

After school, I walked to the carpool line with Tamika and Brad. They were both tall, thin, and attractive, but that was where the similarities ended. Where Tamika was super-emotional and easily excitable, Brad was totally laid back. His high-top sneakers, baggy pants, and warm smile seemed to make everyone feel comfortable around him. He was so likeable, he could probably make friends with a chicken nugget and bring it back to life.

"Girl, I cannot believe The Goon had the nerve to give us homework on the first day of school," Tamika said.

Brad yawned. "What's so tough about finding the name of a character and a song from the musical *CATS*?"

"Taking the time to find out," Tamika shot back.

"I have the CD at home," I offered. "I can call you when I get there."

Brad waved his palm in the air like he was performing a magic trick. "No need, ladies, no need. The answer is... drum roll please...Grizabella and *Memory*."

Tamika's eyes widened. "How do *you* know anything about *CATS*?"

"I love cats," Brad said. "They taste just like bologna." He wore a T-shirt with a portrait of a trumpet player on it. Tamika punched the musician right in the nose.

Brad pretended to be hurt and stumbled to the ground. He was always pulling those kinds of pranks, so Tamika and I ignored him and kept walking.

I couldn't blame Tamika for being surprised that Brad had already done the homework. He wasn't exactly the hard-working, responsible type. Usually, he was the one asking us for the answers.

Brad miraculously recovered and caught up with us as we sat down on a bench.

"Your mom didn't know anything about the master class, huh?" I asked Tamika.

Tamika shrugged. "If she did, she didn't let on."

"Well...I'm definitely auditioning for the musical," I said.

Tamika placed one hand on her hip. "What else is new? Just don't go hogging everything."

Hogging? I'd gotten one lead role at school and shot one commercial. What was I hogging? "Well, you'll audition too, right? And we'll practice together, same as always."

Cinnamon, and one of her clones, strutted in our direction.

"Get ready to bow, people," Tamika whispered out of the side of her mouth. "Here comes Cinnamon Cleaver, the friendly neighborhood Ice Queen."

Cinnamon's voice boomed as she sauntered past. "Mother just got back from a fashion show in Paris. Since she's up on all the latest styles, we'll be heading to the shops at Bal Harbour for lots of new clothes."

I bet people up in Maine could hear her bragging. Being loud was one thing she was good at. That's how she got singing roles when she was younger. Fortunately, other kids were learning to sing louder and better than her. Then her dancing skills had taken off. The problem wasn't that she was so talented.

It was the way she pranced around making sure everyone knew it.

Cinnamon noticed the poster about the show. "Oh, Puerto Rico! The beaches are awesome. And the food is wonderful."

I wanted to plug my ears. My parents were born in Puerto Rico. She wasn't going to get away with acting like a know-it-all just because she went there once, on vacation.

"There's a lot more to Puerto-Rico than the beaches and the food," I told her.

She shot me her well-practiced fake smile. "Of course there is. There's the great hotels and...well...um...the capitol. Oh... I remember, San John."

I smirked. "Yup, San *Juan*."

She gazed upward and placed a finger on her chin like she was concentrating hard. "Oh, and Puerto Rico is exotic, with lots of birds...and frogs...and it's totally surrounded by the ocean... on all five sides...kind of like Florida but with more water around it."

I bit my bottom lip to keep myself from laughing. *Yes, Miss Cleaver, Puerto Rico is an island, and Florida is a Peninsula, not quite an island. Hello, we learned that in fourth grade for Florida Day, but your brain is obviously on vacation... in an exotic place ...that's totally surrounded by the ocean... on all five sides.*

A brand new silver foreign car pulled up. The woman driving it had perfectly smoothed hair and wore huge diamond earrings and a pearl necklace. "Cinnamon, darling, hurry, hurry!"

Cinnamon hopped in beside her and waved to everyone like she was the Queen of England. Only a few of her cronies waved back.

Once the car had pulled away Tamika and I busted out laughing. "Good thing that girl's got talent," Tamika said. "'Cause she was definitely absent when they handed out brains."

Tamika finally quit giggling and took a swig of bottled water.

"Did you ever send your audition CD to the Cyclones?" I asked her.

"I mailed it last week. I'd love to sing at one of their games. I hope they call me."

"I hope so too."

Then the Robinsons' ivory hatchback pulled up. "I can stay after school tomorrow and help you look for an audition song at the library," Tamika said as she and Brad hopped inside the car. "Call me," she hollered from the window as they drove away.

Oops! I didn't get a chance to tell Tamika about sending my audition CD to the Cyclones, too. Oh well. I can fill her in later.

I sat alone, imagining what it would be like to play the lead role in *La Isla Del Encanto*. Being part of a musical would be even better than singing at a football game. I'd seen the Bomba dancers perform wearing their frilly white gowns as they danced to the pounding beat of the drums.

When I'm in the musical, I won't just sing each note in perfect tune, I'll do it while dancing the most amazing version of the Bomba ever seen. I'll make it into the master class, get discovered by a well-known producer, and become a famous entertainer. I'll eat at fancy restaurants, stay in five-star hotels, fly to Europe on my own private jet, ride around New York and Paris in a stretch limo —

Honk! Honk! Honk! My father's beat up convertible pulled up to take me home.

THE SINGING STOMACH

When I got home, several paint cans sat in the foyer. Our house was finally on its way to looking normal. *I only wish Dad would get around to fixing some of the other problems around the house, like the toilet that sounds like a dying frog when you flush it, or the flamingo-shaped knobs on the kitchen cabinets. At least he'll be painting over the wallpaper in my bedroom soon. Although I can't imagine how I'll miss the joy of waking up to a room plastered with tiny green aliens.*

I dropped my backpack on the floor and headed back outside to the car to help Dad carry grocery bags into the house.

Rosa trailed behind clutching her favorite stuffed monkey. "Guess what, Daisy? Daddy is making pickles beaks and goat brain bread for dinner!"

"It's pickled beets and oat bran bread," my father corrected. He had showered and smelled of lime aftershave. His thinning brown hair gleamed while his jeans and T-shirt were freshly washed. *Why couldn't he have looked that way at school today?*

I followed him into the cluttered kitchen to help put things away. Organic plantains, brown rice, seaweed-looking green stuff (*was* it seaweed?), and dried garbanzo beans were in the first bag. *What will I find next, Barf-a-roni?*

My father did most of the cooking, since he worked from home as an online sociology professor. Some of the nutritious meals he cooked turned out okay, but some of them came out looking and tasting kind of weird. My mother rarely cooked since becoming Head Librarian at a public library across town, but we could count on her for holidays and, sometimes, weekends.

Rosa pulled on the hem of my skirt. "We can play hide and seek when you finish with the grossies."

"They're called *groceries*," Dad corrected.

I actually thought Rosa was right, but who was I to correct a brainiac? I unpacked the last bag but didn't see anything resembling 'normal' food. "Thanks for going shopping, Dad," I said out loud. Under my breath I said, "I know I can always count on you to come up with every kid's fantasy snack."

My stomach rumbled as I went up to the privacy of my room and punched in Tamika's number. She sounded excited when she picked up. "I was just about to call you. I overheard my parents talking about the school musical. They said Magoon's nephew works at Entertainment Television and he'll be helping with the master class."

"ETV! They show G-Flo's movies and music videos all the time."

"Yup. Who knows what can happen?"

I could feel my heart beating faster. Landing a part in the musical would take me one step closer to getting into the master class, which would take me one step closer to my dream of becoming the next G-Flo.

"I've just got to land the lead in the musical," I said. "If I don't get ahead of the game now, it'll be hard trying to play catch up later. I am soooo going to end up on ETV."

"What about me?" Tamika almost hollered into the phone.

I sighed. Tamika always went for the smaller roles, and I always cheered her on. She just hadn't managed to land a part yet. "I hope you get a part this year. That would be great. Then we can practice together and help each other."

Tamika was quiet for a minute. "Okay. But you think *I've* got a shot at ETV?"

It was one of those times when I needed to act like a cheerleader just for Tamika. "Who knows how far anyone will go? The field's wide open, right?"

"Sounds good. Anyway, gotta go. *Forceful Fighters* is on tonight and I can't watch TV until all my homework's done."

Phew! Good thing I was able to pull her out of her bad mood. I got up from my bed, straightened a crooked G-Flo poster, and headed toward the door.

Just then, Rosa popped out from hiding beneath the large skirted nightstand next to my bed. "Boogala! Boogala! Boogala! Scared you!"

I stared at her in disbelief.

Rosa placed her hands on her well-fed hips and wiggled them from side to side. "You didn't lock me out, you locked me in."

I groaned. "How long have you been in here?"

Rosa scrunched up her face and pointed her finger at me. "I'm telling what you said about ETV."

I thought fast. "I heard Dad say we're having sugar-free pudding for dessert. You can have mine, if you want."

"Yumma bumma. It's a good thing you're being nice to me or I'd have to give you a slobber kiss."

"What's a slobber kiss?"

"Sometimes spit comes out, on accident, when people kiss you. Then slobber gets all over your cheek. But *I* know how to give slobber kisses on *purpose!*"

The doorbell rang.

Suzanna Delmonico, our neighbor, was bringing her three-year-old son, Benjamin, over so we could watch him while she went to a college class. He usually just ended up following Rosa around doing whatever she did. I opened the door and Benjamin, wearing training pants and a jelly-covered shirt, scurried inside, heading straight toward the bathroom. "I can go potty all by myself," he said.

"Benjamin hasn't had his dinner yet," Suzanna said. "But you know what a good eater he is. I'll pick him up right after class is over. Bye, bye, sweetie," she called after him.

Benjamin flushed the toilet. "Bye, bye, pooh-pooh," he hollered. "Hello thoapy, thoap," he yelled, turning on the faucet. Unfortunately, he always left the door open, so we were stuck hearing every word he uttered.

I went to the kitchen for some juice. As I walked in, I noticed Rosa scrunched into a corner like she was trying to hide. "What's up? Want something to drink?"

"Oh, ot ow," Rosa replied. Her mouth was covered in crumbs and she quickly swallowed whatever she had in it.

"What did you say?" I asked.

"No. Not now," Rosa answered, hopping up to leave. Her pockets bulged and she wore a guilty look on her face. As she hurried past me, the stuff in her pockets spilled out. A dozen of Puerquito's dog biscuits hit the kitchen floor, landing in a heap.

"Here, Puerquito, Puerquito," she called.

"Rosa, don't tell me you've been eating Puerquito's snacks! Gross!"

She frowned, gazing up at me. "They're worse than gross. They're totally yucka-bucka."

I rolled my eyes. "Then why were you eating them?"

Pleeeeease don't tell me they taste better than Dad's cooking!

Rosa shrugged. "To see what I was missing."

———

WE ALL SAT DOWN TO DINNER AFTER MOM GOT HOME FROM THE library. She wore a hot pink dress with matching beaded necklace, headband, and shoes.

"Who would like to say the blessing?" my father asked.

"Me! Me!" said Rosa. She closed her eyes and folded her hands. "Thank you for the wonderful blueberries, even though they're sour. Please help me grow tall, even if I don't eat any vegetables. And please make Daddy's cooking taste yumma bumma. Amen!"

My mother took a bite of her oat bran bread. "What did you learn in kindergarten today, Rosa?"

Rosa stuffed her mouth with blueberries. "I learned that George Washington D.C. was the first President of the United Steaks."

Mom glanced at Benjamin. He sat frowning at his plate of food. "Aren't you going to eat anything, sweetie?"

Benjamin made a sad face as he gazed at Puerquito, who was lounging under the table. I could tell what Benjamin was thinking as he stared longingly at the dog. *Help me, little buddy. Help me.*

Puerquito glanced up as if to say, *You should feel sorry for me. I'm the one stuck eating the scraps.* He put his head back down and stayed where he was.

Benjamin slapped his forehead and covered his face with both hands. My father hurried to the freezer, pulled out a frozen yogurt pop and handed it to our guest.

Benjamin bit into it, banged the table and giggled with happiness, or maybe, relief.

My mother slopped organic butter all over her brown rice. "I got another letter from *Abuelo* today. He sounds like he's ready for the visit he promised."

"Maybe he can come after I finish painting," Dad said. "In a month or two."

"I'll let him know," Mom answered.

Dad started heaping everyone's plate full of spinach salad. I spread my pickled beets out flat, so there wouldn't be much room left on my plate. *Phew! Just in time.* There was only room for a small serving of spinach. I wiggled my plate around, so some of the leaves would fall onto the table and I wouldn't have to eat them.

"Dig in everyone," Dad said. "There's still plenty of salad left. And there are still a couple more bags of greens left in the fridge, so we don't have to worry about running out."

Oh, thank goodness! What would I do if we ever ran out of spinach?

Rosa found a better way of avoiding our ultra-tasty gourmet cuisine. She stood up and started humming a tune. She 'conducted' the music, marching around the table, using her fork as a baton.

"Sit down, Rosa. You'll choke," my mother scolded.

Rosa kept marching. "I haven't yet."

My father, who always drank eight glasses of water a day, quickly guzzled two large tumblers full.

Rosa mimicked him. She drank two full cups. "Oh!" she said. "I learned two more things at school today."

"What were they?" my mother asked.

"How water makes music. Daisy isn't the only one in the family who can do anything. Now you can watch *my* show." Rosa grabbed the edges of her flowing dress and hopped up and down in a circle.

Chug, chug, chug sang the water in her belly as it pounded against her stomach. *Chug, chug, chug* it bellowed as she skipped around the kitchen. *Chug, chug, chug* it chanted as she jumped on her chair.

My parents slapped their knees and giggled.

"What's the other thing you learned, Rosa?" my mom asked.

Rosa stopped jumping. "Oh!" Her hands flew to her mouth. "My class is having music time with Daisy's class tomorrow. Then the professor can meet us and see how talented we are." She grabbed Benjamin's hands and bounced around the kitchen with him.

Oh, great, I thought to myself, *first day Puerquito, second day Rosa. Why does Professor Magoon, of all people, have to witness her crazy stunts?* I ate my food as fast as I could, excused myself, then bolted from the table and headed for the phone. I needed to speak to Tamika right away.

VIVA TO THE DIVA

The next day during music class, the professor stepped from his office and Cinnamon sauntered up, handing him a water bottle. He smiled at her and took a sip. She strolled past everyone, with a smug look on her face, and found a seat on the top riser.

Wow, that was quick. Talk about doing whatever it takes to get in good with old Magoon.

Tamika sat with me on the bottom riser. We wanted to be front and center in case the professor quizzed us on our home-work. I'd listened to the entire CD of *CATS* the night before and memorized most of the song titles and characters. I had to have a chance to clean up my act and make a good impression on him before he met Rosa.

The professor strolled over to the piano and hit Middle C. "Do Re Mi So La," he sang. "What kind of scale am I singing?"

"A pentatonic scale," a girl named Emma yelled out.

"Good. Sing it back to me."

"Do Re Mi So La So Mi Re Do," she sang.

He clapped his hands. "Wonderful. Someone who can sing a pentatonic scale both up and down."

Professor Magoon kept firing all kinds of questions at us

about scales, time signatures, and diaphragmatic breathing. He said he was trying to figure out what we'd already learned so he could fill in the gaps and guide us. Finally, he took a breath and sat down. "You should all bring notebooks to class and take notes."

Who ever heard of taking notes during music? This guy sure means business.

The bell rang, signaling the end of class. He hadn't asked us a thing about *CATS*.

"Please keep your seats," the professor said, glancing at the door. "Another privilege I'd like to offer *all* of you is the role of serving as mentors for one of the kindergarten classes. I've asked them to show us a sample of their talents. This will allow us to see what they know and what they don't so we may be of assistance. I only ask that you model appropriate behavior. Their music time follows yours, making this especially convenient." Rustling sounds came from outside the door. The professor beamed. "Ah, here they are now."

Oh, great! I just hope Rosa doesn't pull one of her crazy stunts before I get a chance to prove myself.

The professor opened the door and bowed like a servant greeting royalty. "Lovely to meet you. Please, come in."

All the children marched in calmly, except for Rosa who hopped like a spastic frog.

She had obviously filled her stomach with water to amaze her friends with her chug-a-lugging. *Talk about a natural born ham.*

Professor Magoon faced the group after they sat down on the carpet in front of us. "Kindergartners, when it is your turn, I would like you to stand up and tell us a little something about yourself. If you'd like to show us a sample of your abilities, you may do so."

He checked the roster. "Where is Cooper Brewer?"

"Here!" yelled a boy wearing bright yellow sneakers on the wrong feet.

The professor waved him to the front of the room.

Cooper trudged forward slowly with his shirttail hanging out of his pants.

Good. The longer he takes, the less time we'll have for Rosa.

When Cooper made it to the front of the room he held up a plastic bag with a tiny tooth inside. "My tooth fell out, see?" He held up a nickel. "The Tooth Fairy brought me a whole quarter, see?"

"When did your tooth fall out?" someone asked.

"Tomorrow," Cooper said, nodding.

"Do you have anything you'd like to show us?" asked the professor.

"I just showed you my tooth!"

The professor sighed. "I noticed you brought your portfolio."

"You mean this?" Cooper reached for a messy folder that held at least fifty pieces of artwork. He pulled out the top sample, holding it up for all to see. "This is my hamster when I brought him home." Cooper flipped to the next picture. "This is my hamster sleeping." He held up the next painting. "This is my hamster playing." Each portrait was a muddy brown blob. "This is my hamster eating...This is my hamster poo—"

"Thank you," the professor interrupted. "I think we get the idea. I see you made good use of the color brown. You may have a seat."

I crossed my fingers. *Pick another boy. Pleeeeease.*

"Let's see." The professor scanned his clipboard. "Will Cassie Cowsill please come up front?"

Phew!

"That's me!" shouted a girl sitting six inches in front of him.

The professor covered one ear, looking startled. "Yes, what do you have for us today, young lady?"

The girl grinned, revealing a large gap of missing teeth. She stood up, smoothed her overalls and faced the audience.

"I likes to watch TV. I watches it before I goes to school in the mornin', when I git home from school, durin' dinner, and before I goes to bed." She stuck a thumb in her mouth and began chomping.

What a cutie!

The professor raised his eyebrows. "Interesting. Anything else you'd like to tell us about yourself?"

"My favorite show is *Forceful Fighters*," she said, leaping into a martial arts stance. "I likes it when the Kung Fu master—"

"Perhaps you'd like to perform something...*artistic* for us," the professor said, running his fingers through his graying hair.

"Yuppers! I'm fixin' to be a actress, so I've been practicin' readin'."

Cassie bent toward his ear and whispered loudly, "I can't read yet, so I got my readin' from TV." She made a serious face and pointed her finger at the class. "Own a new car today with no money down!" she hollered. "Read my lips! Zero down payment! Come to Bargain Billy's and drive away today!" Then she alternated pointing with both hands. "Bad Credit? No Credit? Billy don't care! Come on down to Bargain Billy's!" she said, with a big wave of her arm. "I'll save *you*," she pointed, "money!"

Brad hollered out, "Can Bargain Billy get me a new sports car?"

Yeah, and while he's at it he can get my dad a new convertible.

The professor frowned at Brad then glanced at his gold wristwatch. "Thank you, Cassie. We have time for one more person."

It looks like he's going in alphabetical order. Please, please, please let there be someone else whose last name starts with C.

The professor scanned the list. "Where is...let's see...Rosa De La Cruz?"

Oh, great. Here we go.

Rosa raised her plump hand and hopped in her seat, sending her chestnut curls bouncing. "I can play a scale on the piano."

"Fine." The professor nodded approvingly. "Why don't you find Middle C and start there."

Rosa strode over to the baby grand. She stood for a second toying with the huge bow in her hair. Then she poked her head beneath the piano, the bench, and the professor's seat. "I can't find it," she said.

What?

The sixth-graders seated around me howled with laughter, while I shook my head.

The professor glared at us. His expression softened as he spoke to Rosa. "Why don't you start on whichever note you wish?"

Maybe if I slap a bow the size of Jupiter on my head he'll speak to me like that.

Rosa plopped herself on the piano bench. Her thick fingers plunked out a C Major scale, while her thin voice cracked on almost every note as she sang along.

"C-D-E-F-G-H-I-J."

"H-I-J!" someone yelled. "We got us some new notes!"

The professor scowled. "Sixth-graders, *kindly* observe in which areas the younger students will require assistance. Need I remind you of what we discussed earlier?" He granted Rosa a slight smile. "Thank you, dear."

Rosa hopped off the bench. Her hands went straight to her hips. "I'm not done. I can sing, too."

"Is that right?" The professor raised his eyebrows. "Have at it, then."

Oh great. Just great.

Rosa stood tall and belted out the words to her song. "I long to be a prima donna, donna, donna. I long to shine upon the stage..." she sang, spreading her arms as if she were welcoming guests. "And my figure would look pretty as a page...." Here, she placed her hands on her hips and wiggled them from side to side. "I long to hear them shouting 'viva' to the diva, how very lovely that would be..."

The song went on and she clasped her hands together as if in prayer. "That's what I'm dying for. That's what I'm sighing for. Art is calling...aaaaah ah ah aaaaah, ah ah ahhhhhh..." her voice cracked hideously. She pointed her thumbs to her chest and spoke the last two words. "For me!" As Rosa finished, she threw her arms up in the air like an Olympic gymnast at the end of a routine. "I can whistle it through my nose, too. Wanna hear?"

Some of the sixth-graders clapped along with the kindergartners who 'oohed' and 'aahed' and acted as if Rosa were the diva sensation she had sung about.

Hello! Don't you guys have ears?

The professor stared at her with buggy eyes. "I expected *Itsy Bitsy Spider*, not a Victor Herbert composition."

Rosa shrugged. "Nope. No spiders. We only have ants and roaches at our house."

The professor acted as if he hadn't heard her. "Where did you learn such an advanced song?"

"From my sister. She sings along with an old G-Flo CD she plays all the time. But her voice cracks real bad when she sings it. It's not beautiful sounding like mine."

Oh, you'll be making some beautiful music, all right, when I get a hold of you!

The professor spoke gently. "Ah, yes. I think I remember Gloria Florez doing a classical album. But as far as your sister goes, remember, that's what this school is here for. To help our students learn. Maybe you can persuade her to come to this fine arts magnet as well."

"She *is* here. That's her right there," Rosa said, pointing her fat little finger in my direction.

The professor squinted at me. "I see...I thought the last name had a familiar ring. Your older sister and I have already become acquainted."

I hit him with a stiff smile. *Will anyone notice if I crawl under the risers or escape through a window?*

"Her name's Daisy, but *I'm* the one who's a delicate flower," Rosa continued, pointing her thumb to her chest.

"Indeed." said the professor.

Rosa wagged her finger in the air. "And I heard her say she had to get the lead in the musical, so she can be on ETV and be famous and—"

"I'm sorry, Rosa, but we've run out of time," the professor interrupted. "Thank you, kindergartners, for your lovely visit."

I headed for the door. *I wonder how much trouble I'll be in if I stuff my blabbermouth sister in the trash can head first.*

Cinnamon rushed up behind me, laughing. "With all your experience, you'll be on ETV by the end of the week, I'm sure." A few of the other kids standing nearby laughed along with her.

Our homeroom teacher showed up at the door to lead us back to class. I ignored Cinnamon and followed Mrs. Sandberg.

"You okay?" Tamika whispered, following me out.

"Fine, just fine. No pressure," I told her. "I've just got to come up with a knock out audition song, feed Rosa to Puerquito, and buy a white flag to wave at the Queen of the World."

"Grab a stick and pull off your white sock," Tamika whispered, eyeing Cinnamon.

"She looks ready to charge."

AYYYYY!

Tamika and I stayed after school looking for audition songs in the library. The librarian, Miss Cohen, helped me find a song called *Forever Valentine*. It had on old-fashioned jazzy feel just like the songs from *La Isla Del Encanto* and it would showcase my strong point: my high notes.

Miss Cohen showed Tamika a few tunes for altos, but Tamika had a hard time deciding on a song. I sat down at a table with her to look them over. Cinnamon wandered in a few minutes later, sashaying up to us and peering over our shoulders.

"Oh, good. You girls are smart enough to not try out for lead dancer." She gazed at Tamika. "I wouldn't let her grab all the airtime, though. You'd make a good lead singer if you got the chance."

I'm grabbing all the airtime? Who is she kidding? I'm just starting to get my first whiff of it.

Tamika squinted her eyebrows like she was deep in thought, as she watched Cinnamon slink away. "I think I'll check them all out and see which one works when I get home."

When we were finished in the library, we headed outside to

the vending machines. Cinnamon was leaving as we strode up. She placed a can of diet soda on a wooden tray like she was carrying a royal crown to a European prince. "The professor has to have enough to drink," she said, like she knew his deepest secrets.

We both stared after her. Tamika shook her head. "Talk about trying to worm your way to the top anyway you can."

I sighed. "The rest of us will just have to buckle down and *work* our way to the top."

"Or we could try bringing him stuff, too?" Tamika suggested.

We brought the professor a bottle of water every morning for a week. He always smiled when he took it, but each day, Cinnamon was there ahead of us with a steaming cup of coffee from the teacher's lounge. We tried to see if he needed any help with anything, but Cinnamon had him covered in that department, too. I'd catch her bringing him newspapers, dusting his office, you name it; he definitely didn't need *us*.

———

TAMIKA SLEPT OVER ON FRIDAY NIGHT, SO WE COULD PRACTICE our songs together. I knew if I was going to stand a chance of making it into the advanced class I had to work, work, work, which is what Tamika and I did all night. We didn't go to bed until both of us had our songs memorized.

When I woke up the next morning, I wasn't only surrounded by the little green space men plastered all over my walls, but by my nosy little sister. I caught Rosa searching through my dresser. Talk about no privacy. Tamika was still asleep, so I hopped out of bed and dragged Rosa away from my stuff.

The phone rang as I pulled Rosa into the hallway. My mother's voice echoed from the master bedroom. "*Hola, Papi. ¿Como estás?*...Tired... from your flight...to Miami?"

What's Abuelo doing here? He isn't supposed to visit for another month or so. I ran to listen outside my parent's bedroom. Rosa followed me. We positioned our ears near the crack in the door.

"When did you leave Puerto Rico?....Of course... I'll be right over." My mother hung up the phone. I ran inside my parents' room. "*Abuelo's* here? No way! His room's not ready yet. Nothing in the house is ready yet. What was he thinking?"

My mother fell backwards onto the bed. "Ayyyyyyyyyy! He wasn't supposed to come until Thanksgiving. *Mira que loco.* Ayyyyyyyyyyy!"

Rosa marched in and fell into bed beside her. "Ayyyyyyyy! If he came in a rush, he sure didn't have time to buy me a present. Ayyyyyyyy!"

"*¿Qué voy a hacer?*" Mom asked. "What should I do? There's not an ounce of edible food in this house—not that your father doesn't try. I just don't think seaweed is something your grandfather is used to eating."

Someone was singing in the bathroom. "A,B,C,D, knee, lay, G, H, I, J, J, I have to go pee..."

My mother sat up. "I forgot about Benjamin! Suzanna dropped him off a few minutes ago!"

"Just go," I said. "We'll watch him."

Mom rushed out the door in her nightgown. A few seconds later, she was back. "Where are my black jeans?"

She turned the dirty clothes hamper upside down, scattering clothes all over the floor. When she spotted them, she snatched them up, pulled them on, and headed out. Rosa and I giggled. Mom was still wearing her nightgown over her jeans. She turned back around, grabbed a wrinkled top from the floor, and ran out again.

I didn't often get a chance to stretch out on my parents' king-sized bed, so I leaned back to relax. Rosa found Benjamin, and both of them grabbed the opportunity to jump around on the other half. *So much for peace and quiet.*

Dad barged in a minute later. "Up, up, up! We need all hands on deck if this house is going to be presentable before your grandfather gets here."

I went back to my room to tell Tamika what was going on. "Sorry, but I gotta help clean up. My grandfather showed up at the airport unexpectedly, and we're trying to pull everything together as fast as we can."

She crawled out of her sleeping bag. "Let me get dressed then I can help too."

"You don't need to," I said, throwing a turquoise quilt on my bed and fluffing the silver heart-shaped pillows.

"It'll go quicker, right? Then we'll have more time to practice our songs."

She sure is nice.

I changed out of my pajamas. I'd had them for years, so they were a little babyish with quacking ducks all over them, but they were so stretchy and comfortable I still liked wearing them. And it wasn't like I was growing super-fast. I was what my mother called petite. I wouldn't have worn them if anyone else slept over, but Tamika never teased me about them, so she probably didn't even notice.

Once we were dressed, we helped pick up the house then headed to the kitchen for breakfast.

"I'll be right back," Tamika said, heading upstairs.

The only breakfast food in the cupboard was organic oat flakes and puffed wheat. I sighed as I placed the boxes of cereal on the kitchen table along with two bowls. I felt bad for Tamika, but she had been over my house plenty of times, so she knew what to expect.

Tamika scurried in a minute later carrying her purse. She

poured cereal into the bowls then sat down at the table, hiding behind one of the cereal boxes. She pulled a package of powdered donuts from her purse and handed me a few. "This way, if your father barges in, he'll think we're eating the healthy stuff."

She sure is sneaky. I'm so glad I have her as a friend.

After breakfast, Tamika and I practiced our songs and played a few video games. She decided to leave before *Abuelo* showed up.

A few minutes later the front door opened.

"*Abuelo!*" Rosa screamed, running into his arms.

I gave my grandfather a high-five. His hair had gotten a little grayer since I'd last seen him, but he still wore his old-fashioned cotton Guayabera shirt with the pleats and embroidery down the front. He was definitely not into wearing shorts or sweats. He grabbed me, rubbing his sandpapery whiskers against my cheek. "You decide to dress up for me?" he teased, eyeing my T-shirt and flip-flops.

My father wandered in from the kitchen. "Fernando?"

"Yes, dear," my mother smiled stiffly.

Dad took a deep breath. "You're a brave man. We still have lots of work to do yet."

"We celebrate anyway," *Abuelo* said, pulling a ready-made pan of flan out of a grocery bag. He had obviously asked my mother to stop at the market on the way home.

Mom shrugged then went to the kitchen and brought out bowls and spoons. *Abuelo* sat down at the dining room table and dug in. Rosa and Benjamin raced to the table giggling. Mom and I joined them.

Dad rolled his eyes, trudged into the kitchen, and came out holding a container of low-fat soy milk and a plate of egg salad sandwiches. The egg salad was made using only the egg whites and served on whole grain bread. He placed them on the table next to the flan. "We *try* to eat nutritionally balanced meals in our home."

Flan was a dessert made with egg yolks, evaporated milk, and sugar, so it wasn't exactly low fat or low cholesterol.

Abuelo laughed, pointing to his huge helping of flan. "This has milk and eggs, no?"

Dad opened his mouth like he was going to argue the point but sat down next to me and grabbed a sandwich. He made a face at me as I licked a custard-covered finger.

"What?" I whispered. "You can't expect me to hurt his feelings on his first day here, can you?"

And what about all the milk and eggs I'm packing in? Stay as long as you like, grandpa. I'm happy you're here.

CYCLONE FEVER

Tamika invited me to stay over at her house the following weekend, so we jumped into her in-ground pool with a slide, first
thing on Saturday morning.

"Glad to see you girls finally taking it easy," Tamika's father
said as he paddled past me on a huge floatie shaped like a turtle.

According to Tamika, her father had given her a lecture
about working too hard and not taking time to play, which was
strange considering Sonny Robinson worked long hours selling
real estate. His slogan was: *Don't waste money, just call Sonny.* I
thought it was kind of corny, but some of the other agents'
slogans were even worse.

My mother liked to watch the real estate channel while she
folded clothes. "Just to see what's out there," she'd say. The
slogans came on as the houses appeared on screen. *You can't go
wrong with Lita Wong. Call Neil. He'll cut you a deal.* And my
favorite: *Don't settle for a dumpa. Call Lucy Lumpa.*

Tamika and I took Mr. Robinson's advice that day. We
worked less and played harder. We visited new game sites on her
computer, jumped on the trampoline in her back yard, and
plowed our way through the mall.

By the end of the night we were worn out, so we sat on her bed scanning the latest issue of *Pre-Teen Magic* magazine. Our favorite part was reading the embarrassing moments section and then laughing our guts out. Some kids had gotten themselves into some seriously crazy situations.

I loved relaxing in Tamika's room. Everything matched because it was decorated in a Cyclones theme. Mr. Robinson had played running back for their college football team, so the whole family was totally into them. She'd placed pennants all along the walls in the Cyclone colors of white and royal blue. Her canopy bed was covered in a royal blue satin bedspread. Sheer white curtains flowed down from the top. A royal blue rug in the shape of a football covered the floor, while a royal blue beanbag chair sat in the corner.

Tamika must have noticed me admiring all her stuff because she brought up the Cyclones football team. "I told you I sent my audition CD to them, right?"

"Yeah." I nodded. "I listened to it last time I was here, remember? You did fine, just fine." I didn't know what else to say. She chose an old Broadway ballad that was super hard. I was being honest when I said she did okay. But she did okay, considering the fact that hardly anyone in the entire universe had strong enough pipes to sing it well.

We were still young. Her voice wasn't quite strong enough to hold the notes as long as they needed to be held. While her vocal range was about an octave and a half, which was pretty good for a kid, the notes in the song covered at least two octaves. If she'd asked for my advice before spending all that money to record it in an expensive studio, I would have told her to try an easier song. But she hadn't bothered asking for my opinion.

"I wish they'd call me. The season's already started," Tamika was saying. "How much advance notice do you think they give people? I heard a senior from one of the high schools across town sang at their last home game. I wish I knew her name. I'd call her up and ask."

Wow. I hope they call her since she wants it so bad.

"You know how people who aren't musicians are clueless about how long it takes to learn a song," I told her. "I doubt they give you much notice at all. I bet they'll call you, but at the last minute."

Tamika's shoulders relaxed. "You're right. They probably aren't organized enough to have everyone lined up for the entire season."

I had to steer the conversation away from singing at the stadium. No way could I let it slip that I'd sent in an audition CD, too. Not now. Not with her wanting to sing so badly.

"Does your dad have season tickets? Maybe you'll get to see a game before they call you?"

Tamika shook her head. "Dad always tries to get a hold of *free* tickets. He says he's not going to pay to see a team he didn't get paid to play for. If he ever did get a hold of some, he'd probably take some important client, not me."

"I wish we didn't have school on Monday, so we could keep goofing off," I said, changing the subject. I didn't have to tell her a thing about sending in any audition CD.

The odds were against the Cyclones calling me, so what Tamika didn't know wouldn't hurt her.

EL LOCO FRIED CHICKEN

To entertain my grandfather and give him a chance to eat normal food, my family went out to dinner at his favorite restaurant, *El Loco Fried Chicken*. They served traditional fried chicken and sides as well as fried Latin favorites like *tostones* and *rellenos*. That's what made it loco or crazy.

As soon as we strolled in, my father complained about the 1950s decor. "When's the last time they remodeled this place?" He sighed, slouching in his chair and gawking at the menu. "Don't they have anything even remotely nutritious?"

Abuelo sighed. "We no come for vitamins. We come for taste." He ordered a large family platter of deep-fried everything and coleslaw for Dad. Abuelo, Mom, Rosa, and I munched on our *tostones*, pork rinds, and chicken wings.

Dad sat poking at his coleslaw, which was mostly mayo with microscopic bits of cabbage. His eyes lit up when he spotted the salad bar. "Okay, now they're talking my language," he mumbled, before rushing off.

I grabbed his coleslaw and dug in. *Whatever makes you happy, Dad.*

THE NEXT DAY, WE WERE BACK TO EATING MEALS AT HOME, WHICH meant we were stuck munching on Dad's healthy food. Puerquito sometimes sat beneath Rosa at mealtimes, catching scraps she dropped, but he must have smelled what we were having that night because he was nowhere to be found. Abuelo smiled stiffly, pushing Dad's version of baked *relleno* casserole back and forth on his plate.

"Is everything okay?" Dad asked. "Does it need more onion powder? Basil? Oregano?"

Abuelo squinted like he was thinking. "It could use some more garbage."

My father frowned. Rosa and Mom giggled.

I laughed. *Oops!* "I think he means garlic," I said, getting up and snatching it from the cupboard.

"*Sí, sí.*" Abuelo nodded when I handed it to him.

While my family chattered away, I sat quietly reciting the words to *Forever Valentine* in my mind. *Forever Valentine. Forever Valentine, I'll love you truly, truly, Valentine. We'll always be together, Valentine....*

The ringing phone caused me to jump up from the table. I almost tripped over a stool when Nina from the Miami Cyclones introduced herself. *The Miami Cyclones!* I managed to calm myself enough to understand what Nina was saying. "We listened to the audition CD you sent us and we'd like you to sing *America the Beautiful* at our next home game, if you're available."

"I'm available. Just tell me when and where." I tried to keep myself from jumping up and down.

"Two weeks," Nina said. "Come to the gate a few hours before kick-off. I'll mail you a special badge and toss in some extra tickets, so you can bring some friends."

I hung up the phone. "Yes!" I began hopping around the room.

Everyone had stopped eating to listen. "*¿Qué pasa?*" Abuelo asked.

I shrieked out the details.

"That's wonderful, *mija*," Dad said. "But isn't that the same day as your big audition at school?"

"It's the night before, but I already know *America the Beautiful* by heart, so I won't even need to rehearse before the game. I'll have lots of time to keep practicing for my school audition."

My mom didn't seem convinced. "Hmm. I thought this audition was a big deal. Won't you automatically make it into the advanced class if you get a solo?"

"Nope," I said, shaking my head. "It'll give me a better chance, but there's no guarantee. The master class is for people who prove they're serious about wanting to work in the arts. This is my chance to prove it. If I do both, I'll be covering all my bases."

My parents exchanged glances.

"If you're sure that's what you want to do," Mom said.

"An opportunity I've been waiting for is being handed right to me. I can't exactly pass it up, can I?"

Mom started eating her casserole again. "I still think it's a bit of a gamble, but I see your point."

"Thanks for understanding, Mom," I said, wanting to pinch myself.

———

I couldn't wait to tell Tamika I'd gotten free tickets to the game. The problem was that I hadn't even told her I'd sent in an audition CD, so how was I supposed to tell her how I'd gotten free tickets? And on top of that, she hadn't been called yet either.

At recess the next day I tried to feel the situation out. "Heard anything from the Cyclones?" I asked her as we sat at a picnic table eating pretzels.

She shrugged. "Not yet."

"Singing for them might not be such a big deal, you know. It's not like they pay you or anything." I munched away on a pretzel stick.

Tamika eyed me suspiciously. "How do *you* know they don't pay people?"

I gagged on my pretzel and guzzled some bottled water. "Oh...uh...I... sort of figured."

Oops, oops, and triple oops!

I thought fast. "I'm just saying...you know, some people might not consider it a real gig if they don't pay. Just in case they, uh, sort of, happened to call and ask."

Tamika crossed her arms and made a face. "Daisy De La Cruz, are you jealous? Because it *would* be a big deal if they called me, money or no money."

"No, no...I...I'm just saying..."

Just then Cinnamon strolled past our table. "So, how's your audition song coming along, Tamika? You know, for the musical." She completely ignored me.

Tamika shrugged. "Okay, I guess. I know all the words by heart."

Cinnamon shot a smirk my way then glanced toward Tamika. "It's time you tried out for the lead and not some small part. Maybe that's why you've never snagged a solo. You haven't been aiming high enough. *Some* people need someone to knock them off their high horse. Think about it." She gave Tamika's shoulder a pat, stuck her nose in the air then wandered off.

We watched Cinnamon waltz across the playground and join her cronies. Tamika didn't say much after that, but she kept taking quick looks at me, like I was breaking out in some strange disease.

Why does Cinnamon always have to stick her nose in the middle of everything?

———

I THOUGHT ABOUT CALLING TAMIKA WHEN I GOT HOME, BUT I still didn't have the nerve to fess up about everything.

Maybe I can let something slip out while I'm talking to Brad. Nope. True friends are honest. I blew it by not telling her already. I've got to be honest now.

I broke the news to her on the way to class the next morning.

Tamika glared at me for a few seconds before she spoke. "You sent in an audition CD? After knowing how much I want to sing for them? Are you even a fan? Do you know the names of any of the players? Did *your* father play for them? What business did *you* have auditioning?"

"They're my favorite team. It would be fun to sing for them." I took a deep breath. "I wanted to tell you I'd sent in an audition CD, but you kept saying how much you wanted to sing. I didn't think they'd call me, so I didn't think it would matter whether you knew or not. Anyway, you could still get a call later in the season. It sounds like they only book one game at a time."

Tamika crossed her arms. "Maybe...It's just...well... sometimes I wish you'd back off and give other people a chance. If you hadn't sent in that CD, they might have called me instead."

I sighed. "What's wrong with both of us getting a call? We might both get a chance. That's why I think you should come to the game. You'll know what to expect when they *do* call. I've got enough extra tickets for you to bring Brad *and* your dad."

Tamika stared at the ground and didn't say anything.

I tried again. "We've always done things together. I root for you. You root for me. Sometimes I'll do well and other times you will."

She kicked a rock. Hard. "Girl, when have I ever done well? I'm tired of everyone taking off and leaving me in the dust."

I'd never seen Tamika so upset. "I'm still here. I'm not going anywhere." I waved and grinned, trying to do whatever I could to pull her out of her bad mood. "Just come. You might get a chance to meet some of the players."

Tamika still wouldn't look at me. "I'm not as into that team as I used to be. I'm starting to like some other teams."

Right!

"Okay, whatever," I said and headed to class. *I guess I'll just have to give her some space and let her work this out on her own.*

I gave her some breathing room for a few days and then called her after school.

"If you won't come to the game with me, will you lend me one of your pretty blouses?"

Tamika was silent for a few seconds. "Oh right. You've got to at least *try* and make an effort to look nice."

What's that supposed to mean?

"Well, that's why I was hoping you could help me out. We could both dress up when we go."

"I'm not going. I told you that already."

"Oh, okay...I'll look through my closet then." I didn't need to borrow anything. I was just trying to get her to come, but it was obvious winning her over was not going to be easy.

Tamika clicked her tongue. "Do you have anything nice enough?"

What is wrong with her? She's never been this snappy before, at least not to me. "I've been to a few parties. I've got nice stuff in my closet." I tried to think of something, anything, to cheer her up. "You know the Cyclones might have lost your audition CD. Stuff happens. Maybe you can send them another one with a different song on it."

"Why? What was wrong with my song?" she snapped.

Why did I open my big mouth? "I'm just saying maybe you'd sound even better with a different song, that's all."

"They'll call me if they want me." I pulled the phone away from my ear. Tamika was getting loud. "What do you think? I'm gonna go crawling on my hands and knees begging to sing for them?"

The phone went dead. Or maybe somebody hung up.

GUH MUH NUH

I worked on my song, *Forever Valentine,* every day once I finished my homework. When I asked Tamika about practicing together, she said she was too busy. When I called her to see how things were going, she only gave me one-word answers. All I could do was hope we'd both get parts in the musical so everything would be back to normal between us.

––––––

On the night of the big Cyclone's game, I got to the stadium three hours early. I wore a blue linen pant suit that was dressy but would still keep me cool. Dad dropped me off then headed home to drive everyone else over later.

Nina led me up some stairs to a private booth where I met lots of behind-the-scenes people. I pulled out the accompaniment CD and gave it to the sound guy since I wouldn't be singing with a live band. She led me out to the field and stood me in front of the microphone set up on the sidelines near the fifty-yard line. I ran through the song a couple of times so they could do a sound and mic check. I was amazed at how loud the speakers made me sound. It was like my voice was coming down from the sky.

After practice, Nina had me take a seat in the bleachers near the microphone so I could sit and wait until it was time to sing.

It would have been nice if Tamika had tagged along to keep me company, but as I read through the entire football program, the time seemed to fly by. As the stadium filled I felt my shoulders relaxing, as if singing in front of a large crowd was the most natural thing in the world.

People smiled at me as they passed my seat. Maybe it was just because the Cyclones were a winning team, but everyone around me seemed happy.

Finally, Nina signaled for me to head toward the mic. I stood in front of the huge crowd and belted out the words to *America the Beautiful.* "America! America! God shed His grace on thee and crown thy good with brotherhood from sea to shining sea." My version had an added slow ending with a high note at the end. "From   seeeeea   tooooo   shiiiiiiiinnnnniiiiing seeeeeeeeeeeeeea!"

The crowd cheered. *Woohoo!* I was soaring like an eagle and nothing was going to bring me down. I stood for a moment smiling back at the crowd. Then some guy in the crowd hollered, "Step on it, Ethel. We're waiting for the game!"

I heard a few friendly laughs as I kept smiling and bolted off the field. The guy who hollered at me shrugged his shoulders and waved as I walked past, so I knew he wasn't trying to be mean, he was just a huge football fan.

A few people smiled, waved, or said things like "nice job," as I made my way through the stadium and headed toward my seat. *Talk about fun. Singing live is great. This is exactly what I want to do when I grow up.*

After weaving through the crowd, I finally caught a glimpse of my Dad. He was sitting next to Brad. Once Tamika said she wasn't coming, Brad had invited himself along in her place, which was fine with me since he was a good friend, too. My father had invited our neighbor, Suzanna, and her husband Nathan. Mom and Abuelo had stayed behind with Rosa and Benjamin.

"Great job, Dais," Suzanna said, slapping me with a high-five after I sat down next to my father.

Nathan gave me a thumbs up.

"I've never gotten such loud applause," I said. "I can't believe it was all for me."

Dad leaned over, patting my back. "They were just happy you were done," he teased.

Brad was sitting on the other side of Dad and leaned over to say, "Good job. I never liked that song until now."

"Is Tamika still upset?" I asked him.

Brad seemed a little distracted by the pre-game music the band was playing. "Nah. She's just feeling pressured with all this master class stuff, that's all. She'll get over it."

Phew! That's what I figured. I'm so glad that's all it is.

A few minutes later, I felt a tap on my shoulder. It was a man holding a small video camera. "Hey there, little lady. I'm from WMME TV. I filmed your song and was wondering if you'd let me play it every night as our evening sign-off at the station."

Woohoo! "Of course," I answered.

Dad shrugged. "Fine with me," he said, signing the release form. "Out of curiosity, why'd you pick my daughter?"

The man smirked. "The only other footage we have is from somebody singing the national anthem like 200 years ago."

Whatever. Exposure is exposure. "What time will it come on?" I asked him.

"Two-thirty in the morning," he said. "Starting tonight, if that's okay with you."

"Sounds good." I wiggled with excitement and almost fell

out of my seat. "Go Cyclones!" I kept hollering as the team ran onto the field.

Later that night I stationed myself in front of the television. At 2:30 a.m. on the dot I heard faint noises that sounded like *America the Beautiful*. I pumped up the volume since I could barely hear the words. The sound quality still didn't improve.

The screen was fuzzy, too. I fiddled with different buttons, trying to adjust the picture, but it didn't help. It seemed like the guy had filmed me while standing in a parking lot...ten miles away! I was a tiny speck on the screen. A blob. A crumb. *Great!* I was on television without a doggy suit and you needed a microscope to see me.

I crawled into bed feeling completely fried.

Seven a.m. and the day of my big audition at school came way too soon. I kept yawning as I ironed every wrinkle from my flowing white dress, swept my hair up in a bun and slipped into the highest pair of heels I owned.

The idea had been to look like a Puerto Rican *Bomba* dancer, but after tottering around in my heels I wished I'd gone for the grungy and comfortable G-Flo look.

I'd never felt so tired. I decided a good breakfast might help and headed downstairs.

My father was pouring egg whites into a frying pan when I strode into the kitchen. "Good morning, *nena*."

"Guh muh nuh," was all that came out of my throat. I drank a glass of orange juice and tried to say, 'good morning' again. "Guh muh nuh."

Dad poured himself a cup of herbal tea. "You okay?"

I stood as stiff as a starched shirt and pointed to my throat.

My father hurried over. "*¿Qué pasa?* Are you choking?"

I shook my head, rushed over to the message board on the refrigerator and picked up a marker. *No. I just can't talk,* I wrote.

Dad frowned. "Of course you can't speak with all the

screaming you did last night. What did you think would happen?"

I didn't scream that much, I wrote.

He shook his head. "I told you to go to bed, but no. A twelve-year-old knows better than her father."

Dad felt my forehead. "You don't feel hot, but let's take your temperature just to be sure." He went to the cupboard and pulled out a thermometer.

I shook my head. Hard.

"*¿Qué pasa ahora?*" my father asked. "What now?"

Auditions are today, I wrote.

"Audition or no audition, if a child of mine seems sick, I'm investigating. Open your mouth. I want to see what's going on."

Please, please, please don't be higher than 98.6. Dad pulled out the thermometer. My temperature was normal. *See*, I wrote.

Dad sighed. "*Bueno*, I'll take you to school, but I still don't like it."

Abuelo strolled into the kitchen. He had just finished taking his usual morning walk. He refused to wear shorts or workout clothes even when he exercised, but sported khakis and a short-sleeved cotton shirt. At least he wore sneakers.

He bit into a pastry as Dad filled him in on what was going on. Abuelo shook his fist in the air. "*Sí, sí*. Go for it. You go, grill!"

I'm glad Abuelo understood because I was not missing the audition, no matter what. I remembered reading somewhere that when sopranos got laryngitis they were still able to hit their high notes. And I had plenty of them. I would just rest my voice. I wouldn't utter a single word, or note, until music class. There were several solos up for grabs. I wasn't about to give up so easily.

Once I got to school, keeping quiet proved to be hard. It seemed like every kid in class had a question for me. Whenever anyone did ask me something, I just pointed to my throat and smirked.

"Oh yeah, you're resting your voice," they would usually say.

Not Brad. "What's up?" he asked. "You're not quiet unless something's wrong."

Laryngitis, I scribbled in my notebook.

"I knew it had to be something. Why don't you ask for a make-up audition?"

You know how strict the professor is. I wrote. *What if he says no?*

"Then at least you tried. But this is a big deal, remember? That's all I've been hearing from Tamika."

Fine. I'll ask, I wrote.

I started to sweat when audition time came around. Professor Magoon posted a sign-up sheet in the back of the music room where we wrote down what part we were auditioning for. Cinnamon wrote *lead dancer*, Tamika jotted down *lead vocals*.

Tamika is auditioning for the lead? She usually goes for the small supporting roles.

Hmm.

I wrote down *lead vocals* than wandered up to the front of the room to see the professor.

Can I have a make-up audition? I wrote. *I can't talk.*

He frowned, shook his head and spoke quietly. "I am sorry to have to refuse you, but auditions are like the Olympics. Everyone gets the same amount of time to prepare and that's that. What if someone wasn't ready and wanted more time? It wouldn't be fair to everyone else now, would it?"

I hung my head and took a seat in the back. *He thinks I'm a slouch and didn't prepare. I wish he knew how hard I've been working. Ugh.*

Tamika sat across the room behind Cinnamon.

The professor sat perched on a stool in front of the room.

"Before we begin, I'd like to take this opportunity to wish everyone the best of luck. Now. Who would like to go first?"

Cinnamon's hand shot into the air. Of course it did. She always had to be front and center.

The professor smiled. He seemed perkier than usual. "Marvelous. The dancers will go first today."

Cinnamon stood at the front of the room as music from *The Nutcracker* filled the air.

Her pink tutu bobbed along with her as she moved gracefully to the flowing sounds of the *Flower Waltz*. She didn't dance around the room; she floated. Her motions were smooth and effortless. She finished her audition by turning three pirouettes in a row. People clapped like crazy when she finished.

One spot in the master class down, eleven to go.

A few more dancers auditioned. Some routines were excellent while others were barely passable. No one came close to Cinnamon's expertise. She was definitely going to gloat.

After the dancers finished, Professor Magoon ran his fingers through his graying hair. "Which of our singers would like to go first?"

"Me!" Tamika practically screamed. She jumped out of her seat, jamming her accompaniment CD into the sound system before the professor even had a chance to call on her.

Gospel music played for a few bars before she broke into *Oh, Happy Day*.

A few kids clapped along with the beat. I thought she sang okay until she tried hitting a few high notes near the end. Big mistake. High notes had never been her strong point.

It was typical of Tamika to start out strong and then totally fizzle out. She always got nervous singing in front of a crowd. In third grade, she completely froze up during her big scene in the class play. She just stood there, center stage, like a mummy that had been unearthed. Her mother had to literally vault onto the stage and drag her off.

As she headed back to her seat, people started clapping. I tried catching her eye to shoot her the thumbs up sign, but she didn't even look in my direction. She almost always glanced at me for a sign of approval. As she sat down, Cinnamon gave her a fist bump.

What's up with that? I've never seen her act chummy with Cinnamon before.

Professor Magoon asked who was brave enough to go next. I remembered the magazine article I had read about people being able to sing even if they couldn't talk and raised my hand. Where Tamika's high notes were weak, mine would be loud and strong. At least I told myself they would be. What else could I do but try? I had to try.

I recited the words to myself as I strolled up and grabbed the mic. *Forever Valentine. Forever Valentine, I'll love you truly, truly Valentine. We'll always be together Valentine....*

Professor Magoon sat up straight in his chair.

I placed my accompaniment CD into the stereo. Music from the Big Band Era piped out. I took a deep breath. The words, 'Forever, Valentine', surged from my throat.

If anyone had been snoozing, they were wide-awake now. Tamika was the only person hunched over.

"Forever, Valentiiiiiiiiiine," I sang again. "Uh, luh, yuh, doo, ee, doo, ee, Valentiiiiiiiiiiine. Wah, ah, weh, eee, duh, geh duh, Valentiiiiiiiiiiine...."

On and on I mumbled. My high notes were working fine but my low and medium notes had taken a vacation. *Yikes!* I tried my hardest to sing well, but no such luck. The flowing melody I'd planned on singing now sounded like hideous screeching.

I thought the song would never end. From the looks of the audience, they felt the same way. Brad sat shaking his head.

Tamika quit slouching and a teeny smile eased its way across her brown face. Cinnamon got a wicked gleam in her eye, as if she couldn't wait until recess to start gossiping. Professor Magoon wore a stern look on his face. It wasn't clear if he was angry or concerned.

Halfway through the song, I didn't even bother coming in on cue. It seemed crazy to keep fumbling through the words. I cut off the music, sat down and hung my head.

Rumblings came at me from around the room.

"Talk about nervous!"

"That's what happens when you get a big head!"

"She's never sounded *this* bad before!"

"What happened to her voice?"

I stared straight ahead and didn't look at anybody.

Talk about gullible. Why did I believe everything that silly article said about being able to sing with laryngitis? Being able to croak was more like it. Forget about getting into any kind of advanced class. Unless they're in the market for total wannabes, I don't stand a chance.

My parents realized I was taking a gamble by making the Cyclone's gig seem more important than my audition. Why, oh why didn't I listen to them? I hadn't proved a thing to Professor Magoon or anyone else. What I had proved, once again, was that the only thing I was good at was humiliating myself in public.

CAMP CINNAMON

After I got home from school, I stormed upstairs to my room, sank onto my bed, and replayed the worst audition in history over and over again in my mind. I'd end up in the chorus for sure, which would make it even harder to get chosen for the master class.

Maybe I should volunteer to paint the backdrop so I can hide behind it. Forever.

I picked up a book off my nightstand and began to read. It was a fantasy about some guy with supernatural powers. I tried to concentrate, but the book just reminded me that my dreams were a fantasy.

Why did I scream like a maniac at the Cyclone's game? I don't even like football that much. Why, oh why didn't I listen to my father and go to bed early?

Dad came in to check on me. Rosa followed. "Is she okay?" Rosa whispered.

I shut my eyes, rolled over, and pretended to be asleep. Dad threw a blanket over me. "She may have a cold or some kind of bug."

Rosa's eyes widened. "You mean a beetle or a cricket crawled down inside her?"

"I'll explain later. Let's leave your sister to rest."

Dad knew just as well as I did that I was perfectly fine, at least physically. It was nice of him to play along with me. I didn't want to face anyone. Not yet, anyway.

Abuelo crept in later with a bag of food and a soda from *El Loco Fried Chicken*. I sat up. He knew I wasn't allowed to eat junk food except on special occasions. "Your father ask me to get for you," Abuelo said, feeling my forehead.

Dad must think I'm a total mess if he's using junk food to cheer me up. I was pretty hungry, so I opened the bag and dove in. Abuelo patted my head and left me to finish eating.

Rosa tiptoed back in a few minutes later carrying her precious stuffed monkey. "You can borrow *Monito* for a little while." She leaned in close and whispered, "Then, if the cricket comes out, *Monito* can grab it!" She jumped under the covers. "Daddy said I'm not supposed to bother you. If *you* hear him coming, tap me three times. If *I* hear him coming, tap me twice." Rosa was in a good mood, and it was nice to get more comfort from my family. It wasn't like I had anything better to do so I let her stay.

I must have dozed off for real because the next thing I knew, my room was pitch black and my father was leaning over my bed checking on me again.

"Did anyone call for me?" I squeaked out. My voice was still raspy, and I hadn't even gotten a text from Tamika.

"Nope. Sorry."

I sighed and checked my cell again for texts. Brad had sent me an emoji of a monkey with his hands covering his ears which made me smile and helped to soften the blow, but there was nothing from Tamika. Part of me was hoping she'd call and let me know why she'd decided to try out for lead vocals. *Not that it's a big deal. It's a free world. She can go for what she wants to. It's just that usually she lets me know what's going on. It feels so strange to be kept out of the loop.* The other part of me knew that not hearing from her was a bad sign. A sign I kept pushing to the back of my mind, hoping it would slowly fade away.

———

WHEN I WOKE UP THE NEXT MORNING, MY THROAT FELT BETTER, and I was able to speak. I pulled on my best jeans and sandals. *Whatever happens, I'm going to look pulled-together, as cool as a polar bear in a blizzard. But I've got to see those audition results before anyone else.*

Dad dropped me off at school early, and I raced toward the music room. The results were posted on an outdoor bulletin board encased in glass. Even though I'd rushed to get there, I found myself inching toward the results when they were finally within reach.

A few students hung around chatting. If I wanted my privacy, I had to hustle. My legs felt like heavy sacks of rice when I tried to move, but I dragged them over to the list. Once I reached it, I froze. Only my eyes moved as they scanned the results.

Tamika Robinson was listed under lead vocals. Cinnamon Cleaver made lead dancer.

My name didn't even show up under a minor solo or duet. I spotted the chorus roster. My name showed up at the top of the list. I closed my eyes and made a silent wish: *My name will magically jump to the roster marked soloists.* I opened my eyes. Nothing had changed.

For a minute, I thought I was standing in a heavy fog. It was as if I was watching the sadness from a distance. As if everything was happening to someone else, because it couldn't be happening to me. I'd experienced the same sensation a few years earlier when my cat had died.

Footsteps pounded on the pavement behind me, so I turned away from the list.

"Oh, aren't we looking nice for once." Cinnamon strolled up, read the results and gazed at me. "I'm so sorry you didn't get the lead." She grinned smugly. "Or any solo at all. It's so sad when that happens. Not that I would know. Failure must be soooo depressing. Let's see who else struck out." She flipped her long red curls over her shoulder and glanced back at the list. "Wow! It must be awful when your kid sister gets a solo and you don't."

What? I scanned the list again. Cinnamon pointed to Rosa's name at the bottom of the dance roster. Rosa was listed last, meaning her part was small, but she had a solo.

I stared at the ground. "I've got to go. I don't want to be late." I headed toward the nearest restroom, afraid I'd end up crying in public.

As I leaned against a sink and pressed a damp towel across my forehead, Tamika wandered in. I took a deep breath and turned toward her. "Congratulations. You did a nice job at the audition."

Tamika placed her hands on her hips. "I figured if you wouldn't move over and start sharing the spotlight, I'd just move you on out the way."

What? I felt my chest tighten. "I didn't even start getting leads until last year. Cinnamon is the one who's been hogging everything since day one."

Tamika glared at me. "She's a dancer now. She's not my competition."

"Competition? I thought we were in this together."

She pointed her finger at me. "You didn't even tell me about the audition for the commercial you did. And when you got the part, did you invite me to the shoot so I could maybe meet some people? Sounds like hogging to me."

I took a deep breath. "My agent told me about the audition. But you're right. I could've asked you to come to the shoot. I guess with being excited and everything, I just didn't think."

Tamika stared at me, crossing her arms and breathing heavily. "And I don't think I'll ever forgive you for the Cyclones fiasco. You just went behind my back and auditioned. They still haven't called me."

I shook my head. "They were open auditions. I couldn't tell you because you were being so possessive about it. Like you were the only one who should have sent anything in. We're going to end up competing against each other once in a while. You'll win sometimes, I'll win others, but most of the time neither one of us will win, so I don't see why it's such a big deal. Why can't we just help each other so we'll both end up doing well? Anyway, it's not like I've already made it. I've still got a long way to go."

"Girl, don't you know it!" Tamika's fingers pointed every which way. "Wearing them big ugly suits. You got a *super* long way to go."

My eyes teared up. "Then why are you so mad?"

Tamika scowled. "While you've been on your way, I've been stuck on the sidelines."

"You were the one who got the lead in the musical. I made a total idiot of myself."

"Good. Now you know what it feels like!"

"What?" I let loose and bawled while Tamika ran out.

I'm supposed to give up my dream so she doesn't get hurt if mine comes true and hers doesn't? What kind of a friend expects that?

A few minutes later I blew my nose and headed outside. Other kids were reading the results. I watched Tamika shooting her mouth off with Cinnamon and her gang. *Talk about going over to the enemy!*

Professor Magoon lumbered toward me. He'd been scurrying around frantically all morning. I didn't know why Cinnamon wasn't helping him. Since she had made lead dancer maybe she thought she'd earned her spot in the master class and didn't need to suck up to him anymore, if that was the motivation behind what she'd been doing.

The professor and I made eye contact. I kind of half smiled while he nodded. At least *he* was still acting the same way toward me: lukewarm.

I decided to head toward homeroom, even if it was a little early. Brad stood on the sidewalk nearby. As I walked past him, he fell in step beside me. Good thing he still wanted to be friends, even if Tamika didn't. A friend was what I needed right then.

"So," he said, looking a little uncomfortable.

"Tamika's mad at me," I told him.

Brad nodded. "Yeah, but it'll blow over."

That's what you think.

With Brad being the lighting and scenery type, he didn't have a clue how important the master class was to the rest of us.

"You should see the way *we* pick on each other," Brad was saying. "She's not gonna last long over in Cinnamon's camp, I can tell you that."

"She *has* to talk to you. You're her brother. We just had a huge fight. I don't think it's the same thing."

"A fight? Hmm." Brad furrowed his brows. "If she gets mad enough she *will* hold a grudge. I've already been wracking my brain for ways to get you two back together. I'll have to think even harder now."

So that was it. Brad was sticking around to try and get me and Tamika to make up. He jabbered away about how awesome the Cyclones' game was, but I couldn't focus on much of what he said.

Why does Tamika think we can't be friends and compete against each other? Athletes do it all the time. If being friends with me isn't important enough to her, she can adopt Cinnamon as a sister for all I care! I managed to get a professional gig, and I got it without the help of the school musical. If they think I've been hogging all the gigs, just wait! They haven't seen anything! They are not going to get the best of me. I am soooo getting into that master class, no matter how hard I have to work to get there.

MISS DRUMSTIX

"Aren't you excited about your solo?" I asked Rosa on the ride home from school. She hadn't said a thing about it.

"Whatever," she said, yawning.

So much for kindergarten aspirations.

When we got home I ran inside and sat in front of the TV waiting for *Shaniquah* to start. Brad talked me into watching it because they were doing a show about dealing with disappointment. "It can only help," he had said.

Like I needed comfort. *Hellooooo! I need a break, a role, a gig!* Then I figured since Brad was so easy-going he might know what he was talking about, so I decided to tune in.

"*Shaniquah's ooooonnnnn!*" the jingle chimed from the TV set, as Shaniquah made her way to the stage. "*On our show today we have my good friend, Dr. Jill. What is the best way to deal with disappointment and get going again, Dr. Jill?*"

"*Shaniquah, anyone dealing with loss must get through the first four stages of grief: denial, anger, bargaining, and depression. But the good news is we can come to accept and even embrace our disappointments when we enter the final, yet freeing, stage known as acceptance.*"

"Thank you, Dr. Jill. We'll be back right after these messages."

I searched for the remote to turn off the TV. I'm sure she meant well, but I didn't understand one thing Dr. Jill had said.

"Want a career in movies, fashion, or entertainment?"

I stopped hunting for the remote, sat back down, and watched.

"If the answer is yes, you could be the next Miss Drumstix. You, yes you, could be on television. We're looking for local girls between the ages of twelve and fifteen to represent our fabulous new line of tights, leggings, and hosiery. The first-place winner will wear our fine apparel, while the runner up will be honored with the title of Miss Flamingo and will be at her side as her right wing.

"The third-place winner will receive the honor of being crowned as mascot and will have the incredible privilege of wearing our special Spring Chicken Costume during commercial tapings and appearances. Call 1-800-555-S-T-I-X for information on how you can be the next Miss Drumstix. Bawk! Bawk!"

I texted my agent faster than a chicken can lay an egg. She texted back saying it couldn't hurt to enter and that she'd give them a call and fill me in on the details. It would be great to win or at least place second. A chicken suit wasn't something I'd be willing to wear. *Well...I guess I can be persuaded if the money is good.*

Abuelo wandered in from the hallway. "You looking a little dense lately. You worry about crummercials? I rent a car and drive you wherever you want, okay?" He slipped away before I could answer. I wondered if Abuelo's interest in helping me was just an excuse to get away from my father's healthy cooking, but I wasn't about to question his offer. Anyway, he'd backed me up on my school audition, so it seemed like he understood.

I told Brad about the contest at recess the next day as we sat on the swings, and made him promise not to tell anyone.

"A chicken suit?" he laughed. "Right. Like anyone would want details about how to get stuck wearing *that*."

"I can't win if I don't try. And the chicken suit is for third place." It probably sounded like I was reciting the words of a sweepstakes commercial, but I had to stay even with Cinnamon and Tamika.

"What are you trying to win now?" Cinnamon snuck up behind us. Tamika tagged along, which was starting to become a routine.

"Oh nothing," I answered.

"Look who it is," Brad said, smiling at Tamika. He opened his eyes wide and jerked his head in my direction. He was obviously trying to get Tamika to say 'hi' or something nice to me.

Tamika gave me a dirty look instead. "Keeping information to yourself again?"

"Oh right, Tamika. Like I'm personally hiding every audition announcement." I started breathing harder. "For your information, I heard about the Miss Drumstix contest on TV!"

Tamika and Cinnamon glanced at each other, grinning. "Thanks for sharing," Cinnamon said as they left.

Oops! Stupid! Stupid! Stupid!

Why did Cinnamon, of all people, have to find out about the contest? It was like she needed to prove she was more talented than me, was better than me...Something! *Well, it's a free world. She can audition for whatever she wants to, but then, so can I.*

Brad crossed his arms, looking satisfied. "That didn't go too bad."

I rolled my eyes.

He sighed. "Okay, okay, but at least you know who your competition is."

———

We went to music class later that day.

"It's time to start rehearsing for the musical," said Professor Magoon. "Seeing as most of you will be performing in the chorus, we'll go ahead and start learning the songs."

When he said the word 'chorus' Cinnamon turned around and hit me with a smirk, as if to remind me of the fact that I hadn't gotten a solo.

"Would you help me hand out the sheet music for the first song in the musical, Miss De La Cruz?"

While I made my way down the risers past Cinnamon, she coughed into her hand and said, "Chorus." Tamika giggled, but I ignored their immature jabs. The professor had asked *me* to help him, not them.

While the rest of us went over the song, Cinnamon yawned and acted bored, as if she were the queen and her servants were the ones stuck doing all the work while she relaxed. Other kids had to notice how superior she was acting. It was a wonder she still had any friends.

We continued rehearsing for the musical every time we went to music class and slowly, we began to learn all the songs.

———

Finally the day of the Miss Drumstix contest arrived. On the night of the contest I tried to get my legs to look the best they possibly could. I borrowed my father's electric razor and slathered my legs with cocoa butter to get them nice and shiny. I noticed a lot of pageant contestants had shiny-looking legs.

Abuelo was a little nervous about fighting traffic on a Friday night, but he stepped on the gas when I told him there was an *El Loco Fried Chicken* drive-through on the way.

My hands were sweating like mad when we finally pulled up

to the Dade County Fairgrounds. Before security let me pass through the gate, Abuelo had to sign a release form saying I would fulfill all my duties if I won any of the spots in the contest.

Then some guy handed me a potato sack. "Pull it over your head and wear it before you go backstage so the judges won't know who you are."

"Why can't we just put them on before we go on stage?" I asked.

"They don't want anyone cheating and wandering onto the stage without being covered. The contest is for legs only."

When we finally reached the judging area, they wouldn't let Abuelo come backstage with me. "Contestants only," the man said.

I threw the potato sack over my head and made my way backstage alone. Good thing it was loose and baggy because the material felt scratchy when it got near my skin.

Whoever cut the eyeholes out of the sack obviously hadn't put one on and tried to walk around in it. I wore my mother's red stilettos, so I kept tripping over anything and everything. They were the prettiest sandals in our house, and I figured scarlet shoes would be sure to get noticed.

When I got backstage it was obvious I'd be competing with about fifty other girls, or giant potatoes, because that was what everyone looked like. All I saw around me were huge brown blobs connected to skinny legs, which were connected to feet. I spotted a pair of boat shoes, some brand-new sneakers, and a pair of clogs.

Clogs? Sorry, ladies. They're cute, but they don't exactly show your legs to their best advantage.

I glanced around some more and spotted sandals, sandals, and more sandals, in every color of the rainbow. There were only two other pairs that were red. They were right next to each other. One pair was jewel-studded and fancy. They were probably made by some famous designer. They seemed familiar. I took a good look at the legs that went with them. *Those shapely dancer's legs can only belong to one person: Cinnamon Cleaver.*

The other red sandals were flashy but not over the top. Athletic brown legs went with them. They had to belong to Tamika. And the shoes were brand new. *Copy Cat.*

The one good thing about being stuck wearing a totally dorky sack was that it made it hard to tell who was who. I didn't need the owners of those other red shoes to spot me.

I decided to head over to the other side of the room, and as I did, I heard scuffling noises and a few groans behind me. Some of the girls had tripped and fallen over.

"Who pushed me?" someone asked before starting to cry.

"Yeah, who's tripping people?" another girl said.

One of the girls pulled her sack off her head. "Oh puleeeeese, if I'm going to get killed just for entering a contest, forget it," she said before leaving. She had nice legs.

A few of the other girls who had been pushed followed her out. They were all in great shape and seemed like they might have done well. None of them wore sneakers or clogs.

I glanced around for a grown up. *Hello! Why aren't they around when you need them?*

A minute or two later a woman came in, stuck numbers on our backs, and told us to form a big circle. So I made my way over to the rest of the group. As I moved toward the back of the line, I felt something hook around my leg. I glanced down but too late. I fell face first onto the floor, but managed to break the fall with my hands. Good thing the potato sack was loose and baggy. But my palms hurt, so I stayed on the floor where I landed. While I hadn't seen anything coming toward me, I did see a foot leaving as I fell. The guilty person wore red designer sandals.

I do not believe this! What a royal witch Cinnamon is! She was lucky I was in major pain or I would have grabbed her broomstick, flown after her, poured a bucket of water over her head, and clapped as I watched her melt into the ground.

The woman rushed over to me. "Are you okay, sweetie?" She helped me up.

I dusted myself off and checked my legs. *No scratches, thank goodness!* "I'm fine," I told her.

She had already started herding people onto the stage, so there was no chance to bring the Ice Queen to justice.

I took a few deep breaths to calm down then followed her.

Once we were all on stage, they had us march around once and then stop. Anyone wearing sneakers, boat shoes, or flats got pulled out of line. The girls seemed excited until they were told they were being eliminated. *Fifteen gone, thirty or so left.*

We marched around and stopped again. It felt like we were playing a game of musical chairs. Those wearing one-inch heels were next to go. *Down another dozen or so, leaving about twenty.*

Anyone wearing a closed-toed shoe got kicked out next, leaving about fifteen sandal-wearers. All earth tones were escorted to the door then anyone silly enough to wear white after Labor Day got nixed.

We were down to six contestants. Three black, patent leathers and three red-shoed wonders. A black patent leather made her exit, then another, and then another. Only the red-footed remained. I began to wonder if I had entered a leg contest or a shoe competition.

Then it hit me. I was one of the winners. And Cinnamon and Tamika had placed as well. *But who had won what?*

We circled the stage one last time. I doubted Cinnamon would have the nerve to trip me in full view of everyone, but I took small steps and tried to stay away from her, just in case.

Finally the announcer took the stage. "Okay folks. We've got our winners. Our new Miss Drumstix is... Number Twenty-three. Number twenty-three would you please reveal yourself and join me?"

Cinnamon threw off her potato sack and sashayed over to him while the crowd burst into applause. She flipped her hair behind her shoulders and went straight for the mic. "I'd like to thank the academy, I mean judges, for their insight in choosing me as the winner. My biggest goal during my reign will be — "

"Now for Miss Flamingo, her right wing," the MC interrupted, snatching the mic from the stand and gripping it firmly in his hand. "Number twenty-four, please reveal yourself."

Tamika hurled her potato sack to the floor. *Oh, great! That means I'm the one stuck wearing a chicken suit. This is just what I need, Tamika upstaging me again. She's going to rub it in my face but good.* She stood beaming while the crowd clapped.

The thought of wearing a chicken suit made me want to jump into the crowd and plead insanity. Then I remembered Abuelo had already signed the release form, so I couldn't back out.

"And our new mascot, acquiring the incredible privilege of wearing our wonderful Spring Chicken outfit, is the lovely number thirty-seven!"

Cinnamon and Tamika are not going to get the best of me. Not this time.

I lifted my sack, flung it across my shoulders and twirled it around my neck like a scarf. I fluffed my hair, swung my hips, and strutted across the stage as if I were a supermodel on the runway of a famous designer.

The Ice Queen blasted me with her I'm-so-much-better-than-you smirk, while Tamika didn't even bother looking my way.

"*Bawk! Bawk!*" someone squawked from the audience.

What to do, what to do? Don't let it bother you. Go with the flow, I told myself.

"*Bawk! Baaaaaaaaaaaawk!*" I crowed back even stronger. The crowd went wild. I figured if I was stuck being a chicken, I should at least be a chicken with an attitude!

CHOPPING FOR CHOOSE

The next time we had music class, the professor marched up and down the risers passing out permission slips. "I thought we'd head out to the homeless shelter later in the week for a field trip after school. The Center for the Homeless can always use extra volunteers."

No one seemed too happy about it, but they took permission slips anyway.

When we went to the shelter a few days later, almost everyone in my class had shown up. It seemed like people didn't want to disappoint the professor.

Two policemen stood outside waiting for us. A few kids gasped as they escorted us inside the ancient house. My home, old as it was, seemed like Cinderella's Castle compared to that place.

At least it smelled good. The scent of steaming vegetable soup filled the air as we followed the policemen through the front doors. The common room was spacious with folding chairs placed in rows and a makeshift stage set up alongside the professor's portable keyboard. The walls looked like my father had attacked them with sage green paint. Faded posters of farm animals, flowers, and fruit were tacked to the walls.

I spotted all sorts of people from different age groups. There were older people, toddlers, and everyone in between.

Professor Magoon asked for volunteers from our class to serve in the soup line. I raised my hand along with a boy named Enrique and another kid named Zach.

"Those of you who don't help in the kitchen are free to stay here in the common room to play board games with the residents." The professor didn't seem bothered by the fact only three of us had volunteered, which surprised me. I thought he would have demanded we all fall in line right behind him.

One of the policemen led us to the cafeteria while the other policeman stayed with the rest of the class. Our small group filed past a room full of unmade cots and a lounge decorated with ancient, torn up furniture. The rest of the house wasn't anywhere near as neat as the front room. It didn't seem like anyone had any privacy. *I thought I had it bad with Rosa knowing all my business.*

The door to the women's bathroom stood open. Chipped tiles and outdated sinks were visible, making my bathroom at home look like it should be photographed for one of those fancy home magazines.

Once we reached the cafeteria, things got a little better. The basic white appliances seemed to be in good shape, and the stainless steel countertops and linoleum floor had been scrubbed clean.

After we washed our hands, the staff members put us to work. We grabbed individual-sized milk containers from the refrigerator and placed them in a large metal bucket full of ice. Then we formed an assembly line and made peanut butter and jelly sandwiches. The professor and a staff member served the soup, while Enrique, Zach, and I served sandwiches, milk, juice, and crackers.

We all cleaned up in the kitchen, while the members of the shelter ate lunch. It was hard to make conversation while watching little kids living in such dreary conditions. Zach and Enrique didn't say much, either. When we were finished, we joined the rest of the class and piled back on the bus to head back to school. I sat hoping what we'd just experienced might soften Tamika's attitude toward me. *Seeing a sad situation might make her think about how important it is to have good friends.* I could only wait and hope.

———

"HOW ABOUT TAKING ABUELO TO THE MALL," MOM SAID AS SHE cleared the table after dinner. "It'll be a good excuse to shop. You know how much I love buying new shoes."

I knew, all right. When my mother found a pair she liked, she bought them in red, blue, green...every color she could find. "Okay," I said. "I've already cleaned my room and finished my homework."

My father wandered in from his office. He seemed nervous. "Are you going chopping for choose?" He had obviously overheard us.

Mom planted an affectionate peck on his scruffy, unshaven cheek. "Yes, we're going shopping for shoes. But don't worry. We'll find a good sale." She glanced down at her shiny wristwatch. "How much damage can we do in a few hours?"

We drove to a shopping mall nearby, but Abuelo said we had to put first things first, so we found an ice cream shop, placed our order, and sat down at a table.

Rosa took a huge bite of her dessert. "Mmm, yumma-bumma. Know what?"

"*¿Qué?*" Abuelo asked.

"My friend Mimi, who lives in a department around the corner, is getting a new baby sister. She wants it to have a rhyme name like hers. I told her Dede would be nice. Then her sister can be part of the alphabet."

"I always liked the name Gigi," my mother said. "It sounds so sophisticated. But she can always go with CeCe or Fifi or J.J. or K.K."

I thought for a minute. "There's always Muumuu or Tutu."

Rosa giggled. "Or Doo-Doo or Pooh-Pooh."

"Girls!" My mother scolded.

Rosa crawled up on the table and leaned across it, putting her face nose to nose with my mother's. "Hey, Mom, I think it's time to wax your face again. Your mustache is starting to show."

My mother laughed. "Is it? How about my beard? Is that coming in yet?"

Rosa cocked her head to one side, rubbing her chocolate-covered hands across Mom's face. "No, but you're getting wrinkles near your eyeballs." She slid off the table and sat down with her index finger on her chin. "Hmm. Your face looks old, but your voice sounds young. I don't get it."

Mom glared at Rosa.

I busted out laughing. Then my mother started laughing, too. Abuelo and Rosa shrugged, devouring the rest of their ice cream.

We split up and decided to meet back at the food court an hour later. I found an accessory shop and bought a headband and some chocolate-scented lip gloss. I strolled back to the food court, sat down at a table, and waited for my family. Instead of seeing them, I spotted Cinnamon and Tamika walking toward me. I had tried making eye contact with Tamika all afternoon at school, to give her a smile, but it didn't do any good. She still acted like I didn't exist. So much for hoping our visit to the shelter would influence her in a positive way.

Wasn't I at this same mall just a few short weeks ago with Tamika? We'd had fun trying on perfume and outrageous make up colors. *Why is she doing this to me? To us?* I missed the closeness of our friendship so much; I felt my eyes starting to tear up as I watched her. I pulled myself together and decided not to let her see how hurt I was. What good would it do? She'd already seen me crying the day we had our fight. It hadn't made any difference then. I'd just act like everything was fine. Grabbing my new lip gloss out of the bag, I opened it, and dabbed some on.

"Getting ready for your next big commercial shoot?" Cinnamon's fake laugh drifted in my direction. "Oh, no, you couldn't be. Chickens don't wear lipstick."

I ignored her, fiddling with my new headband.

This time Cinnamon made sure I heard her. She strutted over and got right in my face. "Congratulations on your win. A chicken suit is so...appropriate for you, don't you think?"

Tamika nodded. It stung to watch her taking Cinnamon's side against me. I looked Cinnamon straight in the eyes. "At least *somebody* won fair and square."

Cinnamon pretended to gasp in alarm. "Like I didn't?"

"You know if you did or not," I said, crossing my arms.

She tried to hide her gloating behind acting concerned. "Oh, just so you know, we'll be shooting the first Miss Drumstix commercial next week."

"I know." I nodded my head. "They handed me the information sheet right after the contest."

Tamika remained quiet. She glanced around the mall, like she was having a hard time looking at me.

Cinnamon smirked. "Have you tried on your costume yet? I can't wait to see you in it."

I bet you can't. "Not yet. They're still working on it. But I'm sure it'll be ready in time." I yawned and tried to act like shooting commercials was sooooo routine.

"Oh, and those sandals your dog trashed," Cinnamon preened. "They ended up being my lucky charm. I had to dye them red, but they helped me win the contest."

Oh right. Pushing your competition out of the way didn't help?

Abuelo wandered up, taking a seat beside me. He glanced at Tamika and Cinnamon. "Who are these prissy young ladies?"

"What?" Cinnamon squawked, turning red.

I tried not to laugh. "I think he means *pretty* ladies. He's still learning English."

"Well..." Cinnamon recovered, straightening her designer shirt. "Just get it right next time."

Yeah, grandpa, get it right next time. It's not prissy. It's low-down-dirty-rotten-gloating-cheaters.

I introduced the low-down-dirty-rotten-gloating-cheaters to Abuelo.

"Oh, now I remember," he said, tapping his forehead. "You chicken winners. *Bawk, bawk.*"

Cinnamon and Tamika did not look amused.

Rosa and my mom walked up. "Hi there, stranger," Mom said to Tamika. "I haven't seen you in a while."

I hadn't had the heart to tell Mom what was going on between Tamika and me. Maybe I thought that if I didn't speak about the problem, it wouldn't seem so real and maybe wouldn't hurt so much.

Tamika finally glanced my way, though she spoke to my mother. "I've been busy working on my career, Mrs. D."

Mom opened up a bag and pulled out a glittery blouse she'd bought for me. Cinnamon and Tamika still stood frozen to their spots. I wanted Cinnamon, at least, to leave already, but it wouldn't have been polite to ask her to take a long hike to Brazil.

Cinnamon flashed her fake smile. "That's awfully pretty," she said. Then whispered, "For you."

I took a deep breath to keep from reacting. It didn't seem like anyone else had heard her, but still.

"We'll be seeing you, Mrs. D," Tamika said, switching her shopping bags from one arm to the other.

Cinnamon fluttered her hand in her signature queen-like wave.

"Later graters," said Abuelo.

Cinnamon hit me with another dirty look.

I shrugged. "Oops! His English." They sauntered away, and I breathed a sigh of relief. The blouse my mother had bought me needed something to go with it. I decided to forget about the 'prissy' girls and strolled off to go 'chopping for choose.'

SPRING CHICKEN

Professor Magoon whizzed by me on Monday morning, carrying stacks of sheet music. The travel-style coffee mug dangling from his hand jerked about as he walked. "Would you mind getting me a refill on my coffee, Miss De La Cruz?" He handed me the mug without waiting for an answer. "Cream, no sugar. If anyone asks you why you're in the teacher's lounge, just tell them it's for me. And can you please check my box in the office while you're at it?" He bolted toward the music room with his hair flying every which way.

Why is he picking me out of the crowd? Maybe he remembers Tamika and me bringing him water a few weeks ago. Or maybe it's because I volunteered to help at the shelter. Whatever. At least he noticed me. I just hope he's not in a bad mood.

I checked his box first then went to the teacher's lounge. There was no one there, so I had no trouble getting the coffee and bringing it back to him.

His desk had so many piles of paper and sheet music on top of it the only part of him I could see was his head, which was bent over a thick musical score. He didn't seem nearly as intimidating seated behind all the clutter.

The professor didn't notice me come in so I cleared my throat. He glanced up, said "Thank you, Miss De La Cruz," then went back to marking up his book with a pencil. I didn't see a spot to place the mug, so I kept standing where I was.

He glanced up again. "Is there anything else?" He wore the faintest hint of a smile, as if he found my problem amusing, but he was so involved in whatever he was doing, he obviously didn't even understand the problem.

"Um, your coffee," I said, holding up the mug.

He hit himself on the forehead, jumped up and grabbed the cup. "Forgive me. Of course..." He took a sip of coffee then spewed it out into the trashcan.

"What's wrong?" I asked.

"This creamer tastes like it's been sitting out for days. Where did you get it?"

I gasped. "The counter in the teacher's lounge. It was sitting right next to the sink."

He sighed. "It was probably left out over the weekend so it *has* been sitting out for days. But it's not your fault. How would you know?" He snatched a tissue off a shelf behind him and dabbed at his mouth. "Could you please get me a fresh cup? From now on please use non-dairy powdered creamer, just to be safe."

I nodded. *From now on?*

"Oh, and did you check my box?"

I nodded again. "You had a magazine and a couple of messages."

"Right. Where are they?"

"Where's what?"

"My magazine and my messages."

Oh, he wanted me to bring *him the stuff in his box not just check it. Oops!* Now it was my turn to hit myself in the forehead. "I'll be right back." I took a step out the door.

"Miss De La Cruz?"

"Yes?"

"My coffee mug," the professor said, holding it up. "And don't forget to dump out the old coffee before pouring in the new."

Right! Like I'm an airhead and I'd forget.

As soon as I took the cup from him, he went right back to marking up the score and humming to himself.

What a noodle-brained nutcase!

After bringing the professor a new cup of coffee and the stuff from his box, I headed to homeroom. Something told me that after winning the Miss Drumstix pageant, Cinnamon's confidence was up and her gossip machine of a mouth was ready to roll...right over me.

I didn't hear a peep from her all morning. Art class went okay, so I got ready to be verbally trounced at recess. On my way outside, I heard her voice. I stopped near a window in the hallway to peek out and listen. She was sitting at a picnic table with Tamika and some of her other clones.

"Pajamas with little quacking ducks all over them?" Cinnamon said. "They sound like they were custom made just for her."

Tamika, you snitch! I can't believe you're telling everyone what I wear to bed!

The kids sitting near her roared with laughter.

I held my head up, marched outside, and strolled right past Cinnamon's picnic table like I had nothing better to do but wander around smelling the grass and flowers.

Out of the corner of my eye I caught her looking at me. "Oh, Daisy," she giggled. "We heard about your unique pajamas. Quacking ducks are almost like squawking chickens. A little babyish, don't you think? Next thing you know, you'll pull out a bottle and start sucking."

I glared straight at Tamika. "For the record, I *do* drink from a bottle." I pulled a Miami Porpoise sports bottle out of my bag and took a long swig right in front of them all.

The kids sitting at the table cracked up all over again. "Good one, Dais," Enrique said. Cinnamon and Tamika were the only ones not laughing.

———

We shot the Miss Drumstix commercial on location at their superstore. Cinnamon and Tamika pranced around like queens in their glittery stockings and cute little skirts while I was stuck wearing a beak, plastic bird feet and huge floppy wings. They wore wings, too. But they weren't clumsy and feathery like mine. Theirs were more like fairy wings. Cinnamon wore silvery ones and Tamika's were peachy-pink. Soothing flute and harp music floated through the air.

The owner of the store, Rita Hoffman, wore a flowing skirt and leotard as well. "This is a work-in-progress, so any ideas you girls have are welcome," she told us.

Cinnamon danced around the set with her wings. She made them glide and soar in time to the music. "What about some dancing?"

Miss Hoffman's eyes lit up. "That's a nice idea. Can Miss Flamingo dance along with you?"

Cinnamon started dancing again while Tamika followed her movements. Soon both were gliding in unison to the flowing music.

Miss Hoffman crossed her arms and stared at me. "Okay, what are we going to do with you?"

She had given us some lines to memorize, but wasn't clear about who would be saying them. "I can be the one to speak—"

"Why don't you have her dance along with us?" Cinnamon asked.

Miss Hoffman nodded. "Okay, let's try it."

Are you kidding me? In this getup?

I wasn't much of a dancer, and Cinnamon knew it. Even if I did know any good moves it was almost impossible to walk in my chicken suit, much less dance in it, but I knew I had to try.

As Cinnamon and Tamika danced, I plodded behind them flapping my wings, trying my best to look graceful, but failing miserably. I stumbled during one of the turns. I couldn't keep up with their graceful movements while wearing such bulky clothing. I was sure I looked as clumsy as I felt.

Cinnamon stopped suddenly and frowned. "This isn't working."

Miss Hoffman sighed. "No, it isn't."

"Why do we need a mascot, anyway?" Cinnamon asked. "This is such an elegant store. This dumpy chicken thing just doesn't fit in with this incredible atmosphere."

I tried giving my two cents again. "Maybe I can say the—"

"Chicken's don't speak, they squawk," Tamika cut in. "I've heard her." She turned toward Miss Hoffman. "She's a fantastic squawker, trust me." She put her hand on her hip and grinned like she was paying me this huge compliment.

"Wonderful!" Miss Hoffman said, clapping her hands. "Let's hear it."

"But I want to say..."

Miss Hoffman raised her eyebrows.

"Bawk," I whispered.

"Don't be shy," Cinnamon said, sweetly.

"Yeah, belt it out," Tamika said, like a cheerleader rooting for me.

"Bawk," I said a little louder.

Miss Hoffman smiled. "I remember you. You were so spunky

and full of life at the contest. Do it just like that. Come on, there's nothing to be afraid of."

Oh, yeah? What about the vultures in disguise standing right next to you? I can't believe how mean Tamika is acting. The old Tamika would've fought for me. If she was still my friend, I would have been wearing a robe and a crown by now instead of this dorky chicken suit.

Wishing for the old days wasn't going to get me anywhere, so I sucked up my pride. I had to. "Baaaaaawwwwwwwk, Baaaaaaaaaaaaawwwwwwwk!" I crowed.

Cinnamon and Tamika hopped around clapping.

I wanted to sit on them until they hatched into decent humanoid life forms.

Miss Hoffman beamed. "Fabulous, just fabulous!"

I am sooo doing more than clucking like a chicken. "What if I say the lines before squawking?"

"That won't work," Tamika said.

"Nope, too awkward," Cinnamon added. "We can do it."

They jumped right in, reciting the lines perfectly.

"That's it!" said Miss Hoffman. "You two girls dance then say your lines and we'll end with one big squawk. Okay? Let's shoot it!"

During filming, I took a humongous breath and squawked as long as I could. I figured I'd get more airtime that way. I still didn't know if the exposure would help me, but a contract had been signed and the money was good.

As I watched Tamika and Cinnamon strutting their stuff, I vowed to snatch a spot in the master class by proving I was a serious performer. I just had to find a different gig to prove it.

BIG BAD HAIR

I spent the weekend finishing all my homework, seeing the latest animated movie at the theater, and helping babysit Rosa and Benjamin. But then it was time to head back to school on Monday morning.

"Daisy's no competition anymore. Unless you're auditioning for the part of a farm animal." I heard Cinnamon spouting off again as she stood with Tamika and her other cronies. "No matter how hard she tries, she'll never grab a spot in the master class."

I spotted Brad and a couple of other stagehands nearby. Unfortunately, I had to walk past Cinnamon's gang to get there. "*Bawk, bawk*," squawked Enrique as I wandered past.

Don't these people have lives? They are soooo not going to get the best of me.

"No way, Enrique," I corrected. "You've got to do it right, from deep inside your lungs, like this." I took a huge breath. "*Bawk Baaaaaaaaaaawwwwk!* See? It's all in the gut."

Everybody but Cinnamon and Tamika laughed, but Tamika seemed like she was having a hard time stifling a smile.

Cinnamon glared at Enrique.

"What?" he said. "I like her. She's fun."

Way to go, Enrique! It's about time someone else stood up to the Ice Queen.

———

As expected, I was the one getting the professor coffee or water most mornings. He had started off by asking for things when he spotted me around campus, but I ended up checking on him every day out of habit. At first, I avoided him, thinking the way he treated me like a human being after the sour milk incident was just a fluke. I was afraid to make mistakes because I thought I'd get eaten alive, but as it turned out he wasn't so bad one-on-one. It was starting to become clear that the professor wasn't mean; he was tough. And mean and tough weren't the same thing. Mean was mean. Tough just meant having high standards.

Besides checking his box and *bringing* him what was in it, he gave me other odd jobs like unpacking music books and placing them on shelves. He also let me work on his cluttered desk. I filed all the stacks of sheet music covering it, so he was finally able to have some real workspace.

His office door was always open, so other sixth graders, or teachers, popped in and out fairly often to pay a visit. Most of the time Brad or one of the other behind-the-scenes types tagged along with me. When it was just the professor and me, we worked silently. But sometimes he'd tell me about experiences he'd had growing up on a farm in Scotland or share a crazy story about making his way as a vocalist in Europe.

"What do your parents think about your performing ambitions?" he asked me out of the blue one morning.

I glanced up from my shelving. "It doesn't matter what I do

as long as I go to college. They want me to be able to get a good job in case this music stuff doesn't work out."

"Hmm. Sound advice indeed," he said and went back to scribbling in his plan book. "Oh," he said like he was suddenly remembering something important. "Not that I don't think you have a shot at success. But one never knows what will happen, even with the best training and intentions. That was also the motto of my parents, and it has a bit of truth to it, as it turns out."

I took a chance and asked *him* a question. "Were *your* parents supportive?"

He sighed. "My family ran a sheep farm. Farming was safe. Secure. They thought I was such a dreamer with all my talk of London, New York, Paris. I couldn't bear to think my greatest achievement in life would be providing the world with one more wool sweater. No. I wanted more."

Wow! We are so much alike.

"Not that there's anything wrong with sheep farming, but...I let my younger brothers tend to the family business. They're quite happy with it, actually."

The early bell rang, and the professor hit me with his signature half-smile and went back to work.

I grabbed my backpack and headed out the door toward homeroom.

I knew if I was going to make it into the master class, I had to land a gig where I got to play something other than a squawking chicken. I didn't exactly seem like a serious performer in that getup.

My agent sent me an email about a new, locally made, kid's shampoo. They were looking for a spokesperson, and auditions would be held the following Saturday morning at a local TV station.

I didn't tell anyone about it. Not even Brad. If he knew about it, he might slip up and tell someone. Then that someone would tell someone else. All I needed was for half the school to show up and make the competition even harder.

On the morning of the audition, I washed my hair and left a little conditioner in it just like Conchita, my hairstylist, told me to. I blew it dry with a diffuser and used about half a can of hair spray to hold it in place.

When I got to the studio there were at least sixty people waiting to audition. Kids were reading, eating, talking on cell phones... I noticed a girl in the corner with her back to every-one, who fluffed her hair like every twenty seconds. She moved to let someone go by.

Oh great. It's Cinnamon. At least Tamika's not with her.

A boy with a mass of golden curls sauntered inside. When he turned toward me, I recognized him as one of the boys in Mrs. Blake's sixth-grade class at school. His name was Ashton but he looked just like Goldilocks would if she were a boy, so that ended up becoming his nickname. Some other sixth graders from my school that hadn't made solos were there, too. Like me, they were probably hoping to snatch a spot in the master class any way they could.

The receptionist handed out copies of the script, and soon the auditions began. The first few kids to arrive were called to the back room, but they came out a few minutes later. When it was Cinnamon's turn, she went in, but didn't return. Goldilocks was called in and like Cinnamon, he never came out.

My turn finally came. I marched back to a huge room, sat on a stool and read the lines off cue cards. "Tired of flat, lifeless hair?" I frowned. "Now imagine the fullest, most lustrous hair you've ever seen." I shook my long tresses out. "Full, fabulous, feathery hair can be yours with Fluffy-Head shampoo." I ran my fingers through my hair.

A stagehand rolled out a large fan that made my hair blow

out behind me. "Don't be a flathead, be a Fluffy-Head instead. Use Fluffy-Head shampoo. It's guaranteed to keep your hair perfect and in place."

I got called back to the room where Cinnamon and Goldilocks waited. Cinnamon treated me like a total stranger. She kept her nose plastered inside a fashion magazine. Goldilocks didn't know me well, but at least he glanced up and nodded at me when I came in, then went back to playing a game on his cell phone. I was glad my mother handed me a book before I left because I sat in that tiny room reading until every single kid had auditioned.

A few others got called back to the waiting room. We all had to read through our lines again. Goldilocks went first. His hair barely reached his shoulders, so it didn't take him much time to pull his fingers through it. When he finished, the director shook her head. "Thanks anyway."

Goldilocks frowned as he trudged out.

The director had me go next. I performed almost the same audition I did earlier. The fan might have blown my hair in another direction, but that would have been the only difference.

"Wait here and have a seat," she said.

The four other kids who were called back read through their lines again. None of them were asked to stay.

Cinnamon went last. When she shook her hair out, it was so long and thick, people up in Georgia felt the breeze from it. And when she ran her fingers through it, instead of it taking seconds, it took weeks. The crew and I sat there twiddling our thumbs while we waited for her to finish. But we all sat up and took notice when she pulled her fingers through her last few inches of hair. As she recited the words, "It's guaranteed to keep your hair perfect and in place," a large wad of curls fell off her head and onto the floor.

"I hate it when that happens," Cinnamon said, giggling.

Why is she laughing about her hair falling out?

Then something even weirder happened.

The director marched over and giggled along with her. "I know what you mean, honey bunch. We've got to find you some stronger hairpins," she said, pinning Cinnamon's hair back onto her head.

Oh my, gosh! Cinnamon uses a hairpiece to make her hair look thicker! That's the secret to her super thick mane. It isn't all hers. But why is the director laughing along with her?

I thought for sure Cinnamon would be disqualified, but the staff people acted like that kind of thing happened all the time. Maybe it did.

How unfair! How totally, unbelievably unfair!

No one had to tell me to leave. I stood up, waving 'goodbye' to the director.

She smiled back and mouthed 'sorry' as I turned to go.

I didn't have to look at Cinnamon to know how she took the news of her win. They could hear her ecstatic yelping up in Tallahassee.

JUNGLE FEVER

A few weeks later, the professor decided to take us on another field trip to the homeless shelter after school.

This time when he asked for volunteers to help in the kitchen, I grabbed a hold of Brad's arm and raised it for him. Then he grabbed hold of a couple of the other scenery and lighting type guys and held their hands up. I glanced over at a girl named Emma and she came over and stood next to me. Zach and Enrique volunteered again, too. It was encouraging to see our small group of kitchen helpers double in size from four to eight.

When we went back to the kitchen this time, we made a huge salad from vegetables donated from the private gardens of various members of the community. All the students washed and scrubbed the vegetables, while the adult volunteers chopped them. We all helped to dish the salad onto plates and then top them with tuna salad and boiled eggs. I was tired when we were finished, but it was a good kind of tired.

As the residents went through the line to get their food, I noticed that some of the older women's house dresses seemed a little worn and some of the toddlers were wearing clothes and shoes that didn't quite fit.

I thought about what I could do to help them. Rosa wore dresses most of the time, so she had all kinds of shorts, tops, and sneakers just sitting in her closet. Benjamin was growing up fast. Suzanna wouldn't mind donating stuff he'd outgrown and didn't wear anymore. My next-door neighbor, Mrs. Miller, always dressed well. Maybe she might have some things she could give away. I decided to talk with each person and see what I could collect to bring with me next time we went to the shelter.

———

"PLEASE CALL TAMIKA AND MAKE UP WITH HER," BRAD BEGGED ME at recess the next day. "Everything is designer this, designer that. She's driving me nuts. She roams around the house saying, 'Where's my Italian leather bag?'" He spoke in a high-pitched voice then pranced around pretending he was wearing high heels and carrying a purse. "'Have you seen my special sunglasses? Who took my Melvins? Or my Billys, or Bobs, or Uncle Sams?'" He finally stopped to take a breath. "We have got to get her away from Cinnamon."

I wish! But I'm not making the first move. Not after how she's been treating me.

I shook my head. "She was the one who ended the friendship, not me."

Brad fell to the ground, wiggling and writhing like he was dying a slow and miserable death. "Heeeeeeeeelp meeeeeeeeeeeeeeeeeeee!"

Cinnamon bugged me, too. Especially since I'd gotten my gigs fair and square. But I was not losing sight of my goal just because of that gloating, cheating, weasel. Tamika would just have to wake up and see Cinnamon for what she was.

———

MY AGENT FOUND OUT ABOUT A LOCAL AMUSEMENT PARK OPENING near us. The local TV affiliate was looking for a kid to do a voice over for them. Whoever was chosen would have their voice dubbed over pre-recorded footage of the amusement park. Only their voice would be used if they landed the gig. I decided to audition for it. Any performing experience was better than nothing.

When Abuelo and I entered the studio, only a handful of kids sat waiting. Tamika was one of them. She glanced up from her cell phone when I walked by, but she didn't say anything, so I didn't either. Goldilocks was the only other kid I recognized. At least he flashed me a smile when I walked past.

Since there were so few of us, the sound guy brought us all to the sound booth at the same time and handed out copies of the script. Tamika and I ended up sitting right next to each other. She volunteered to go first. "Polly Penguin's Party Palace is a great place for food and fun," she spat into the mic.

"Where's that chirping sound coming from?" the sound guy said. "Those darn crickets." He left the sound booth with a scowl on his face.

I stole a glance at Tamika. Her reading hadn't gone well, and her lack of experience was showing. Maybe she'd let me give her some tips.

"Take a picture, it'll last longer," she snapped.

All this time being mad at me and she comes up with a line that's older than Abuelo?

I took a deep breath. "You're popping your Ps," I whispered.

Her eyes widened. "Popping my Pees? Girl, do not tell me I'm so nervous I wet my pants!" she said, checking her lap.

I sighed. "You pop your Ps or Ts or Ds when you get too close to the mic or speak too loud. It messes up the sound. If you back away from the mic a little that should help."

"Oh, right." She rolled her eyes. "Like I'm gonna trust *you*."

"Never mind." I shook my head. Why waste my time telling her my agent had given me tips for speaking into a microphone before I auditioned for the *Stink-Away* commercial? If she didn't know by now that tripping people up on purpose wasn't my style then too bad for her. She'd obviously been hanging around people like Cinnamon Cleaver way too long.

The sound guy lumbered back into the booth. "Couldn't find the little guy. Oh well. Let's try it again."

Squeaky noises blasted from the microphone as Tamika repeated her lines and popped her Ps just like the last time.

The sound guy shook his head. "You're popping your Ps. That's what's causing all the feedback. I wish they'd get us decent mics with filters. I'll let you try it one more time, but this time back away from the mic a little."

See? What'd I tell you?

"Polly...Penguins...Party...Palace..." Tamika recited the words so carefully, she ended up speaking in a monotone without any feeling.

The sound guy made a face. "Sorry. I've got to let these other kids have a chance. Maybe next time."

Tamika frowned as she stood up and headed back toward the lobby.

The younger boys read through their lines. They either popped their Ps or didn't speak with enough feeling.

When it was my turn, I spoke quietly because I was afraid of making popping noises, too. I ended up doing okay, but not great. The sound guy said he'd give me one more chance after listening to the last person.

Goldilocks went last and spoke his lines perfectly. I tried

again, but Goldilocks ended up getting the gig. There were no hard feelings though, and we headed out to the lobby together.

Tamika was still sitting out front, waiting for her ride, frowning. She didn't look up or say anything to anyone. It was like she was in her own sad little world.

I shrugged and left with Abuelo. So much for trying to make a little bit of peace with Tamika. She obviously wanted to keep the war going.

The following Saturday there was an open casting call for a new department store called Jungle Fever. Auditions weren't until noon, so I had plenty of time to prepare.

I went upstairs and knocked on Abuelo's bedroom door to ask him if he'd drive me over. Crumpling noises, like someone was scrunching up a candy bar wrapper, were coming from inside. When he opened the door, I noticed chocolate crumbs around the edges of his mouth. He was obviously eating his junk food in secret.

We got to the Jungle Fever store well before noon. I wore a zebra print headband and a safari style shirt. They were going to let everyone audition on camera and then choose their favorite takes, which would then be shown on statewide television.

Hannah, the woman in charge, asked that our guardians sign release forms granting permission for us to work with trained animals and granting Jungle Fever permission to use our audition footage however they wanted to. So Abuelo sat next to me and scribbled away.

Cinnamon strolled in wearing leopard print from head to toe. Tamika tagged along behind her. She wore a mishmash of animal prints that clashed. Both of their mothers followed them inside, signed the release forms, then left.

By noon, the line snaked out the door. The audition information stated that all we needed to do was to smile at the camera and say something nice about the jungle. Some people decided to take things a step further. Kids were dressed up like animals and some of the grown-ups wore costumes like tribal warriors. There were a few kids I knew, but it seemed like the number of people auditioning from my school, for any kind of gig, was shrinking from week to week.

Hannah led us to the back of the store. A light blue, plastic shower curtain hung from the ceiling with tropical plants arranged in front of it. Cages holding various exotic animals sat off to the side.

A pretty teenager was the first person in line. Hannah positioned her in front of the camera, while Loopy Louie, the animal trainer, placed a colorful bird on her shoulder.

The cameraman put on his headphones. "Ready? Three, Two, One...," he pointed his index finger at her.

The girl said her line. "I always get jungle fever when I shop at the mall." The bird fluttered its large wings as a huge roar blasted over the sound system.

The cameraman removed his headphones. "Good job. Next."

Hannah led a five-year-old boy to the camera, while Loopy Louie guided a chimp over. The boy and the chimp stood face-to-face looking at each other. Finally, the boy giggled into the camera without saying a word.

A woman with a toddler went next. "We just love the jungle," they said, and roared along with the soundtrack.

When it was my turn I caught sight of Cinnamon watching. She glared at me like she was hoping they'd bring out a grizzly bear for me to work with. Tamika had her arms crossed and was gazing the other way, like she couldn't have cared less. Part of me wanted to bust out crying because of the way she kept acting, but I knew I had to stay in control.

I stood calmly waiting until Loopy Louie pulled out a huge green snake and draped it over my shoulders. It felt creepy at first, but once I realized its mouth was taped shut, my shoulders relaxed. "I have a bad case of jungle fever," I said. Then I lifted the snake above my head and spun around in a circle while the roar blasted over the sound system.

Cinnamon and Tamika both shot me looks that said, "You stunk." Oh well. Even if I did, I had tried my best, and that was all I could do.

I watched a few more auditions. Loopy Louie guided all kinds of animals out for people to hold or stand next to as they said their lines. He brought out a turtle, a fox, a Savannah Cat, a hedgehog, and a disgusting insect called a Madagascar hissing cockroach.

As people continued auditioning, some got scared of the roar and then laughed. Others messed up their lines and giggled. Soon, everyone who auditioned was laughing and having a good time.

When it was Cinnamon's turn, Hannah had her sit on a stool. Loopy Louie brought the chimp out again and placed it next to her on another stool. The chimp immediately went for Cinnamon's hair, touching and sniffing it. *"Eee eee eee! Ah! Aaaah!"*

Cinnamon sat stiffly, staring straight ahead. She probably wanted to say her lines and rush out of there fast, but the cameraman was busy adjusting his camera. The chimp gently stroked Cinnamon's hair, *"Aaaah! Aaaah!"*

"Ready?" the cameraman asked her. She nodded. "Three, Two, One..." He pointed.

"I always get a little crazy," she said, as the chimp patted her hair again. "When I shop at—" The chimp looped a finger around one of her curls and yanked hard, pulling off her hairpiece. He jumped off his stool, placed the hair on his own head, and scampered down the aisle toward men's wear. Cinnamon smiled for the camera, finished her line by saying, "Jungle

Fever," and chased after him. The camera kept rolling as the cameraman followed them.

I caught Tamika's eye and we both cracked up. It reminded me of times we'd laughed our heads off watching funny movies together. This was kind of like that with everyone giggling and pointing.

"Wasn't that one of your prissy friends?" Abuelo asked, taking pictures with his phone.

"A hairpiece?" A man with thinning hair held his stomach, laughing. "All these bald men around, and that girl thinks she needs a hairpiece?"

Loopy Louie caught the chimp, the cameraman returned, and Cinnamon found her way back, too. But she had a lot less hair. When the cameraman got everything back in place, Cinnamon sashayed up to him. "Can we try it again? I'm not sure I said my lines quite right."

He shook his head. "One audition per customer. And with so many people trying out, I need to stick to the rules." He turned back to his camera.

She clasped her hands like she was about to kneel in prayer. "Oh, please, pretty please, with cherries on top!"

The cameraman had been patient and pleasant with everyone so far. "Be happy with what I shot...or... I can delete it. Next!"

Cinnamon stormed off and didn't even wait to watch Tamika's audition. When Loopy Louie placed a Madagascar hissing cockroach on Tamika's outstretched hand, I laughed so hard I had to cover my mouth.

"Three, two, one..." The cameraman pointed.

Tamika gazed down at the cockroach like it was about to swallow her alive. "I just, uh, wanted to say." It made a loud hissing noise. "Get...this...thing...off...me!"

Oops! Something told me she wouldn't be making the cut.

A FEW DAYS LATER, WHILE I WAS WATCHING *FORCEFUL FIGHTERS*, the Jungle Fever commercial came on. It opened with a woman holding her toddler then showed a few people laughing their heads off with turtles, foxes, and birds. It closed with a shot of Cinnamon chasing the chimp and then playing a game of tug of war with it, using her 'hair' as the rope. I had a feeling she wouldn't be gloating anytime soon.

At carpool drop-off the next day, Cinnamon stood chattering away with her cronies. She had combed her hair into a new style —a long, rather skimpy, French braid.

Everyone was whispering and staring at her when Enrique strolled up to her and put his face near her hair. "Eee-eee-aah-aah-ooh-ooh." He rubbed his armpits and flailed his arms over his head.

Cinnamon sauntered past him with her nose in the air. "You're just jealous."

Enrique burst out laughing. "Yeah, I'm jealous a chimp didn't pull off *my* hair. Eee-eee-eee."

Hmmm. I wonder how Enrique, and everyone else, found out about the monkey pulling Cinnamon's hairpiece off. They didn't show that part on TV. Tamika and I were the only kids there from school. I didn't blab, so Tamika must have. Interesting.

Our guardians had all signed release forms giving the Jungle Fever stores permission to use our audition footage however they saw fit, so I'm sure Cinnamon would have clawed her way out of the contract if she could have. She probably couldn't wait to get a new gig to change her image, but I was determined to stay one step ahead of her.

BROCCO BRUSH

As the professor and I sorted through piles of paperwork one morning before school, he told me what it was like the first time he'd had to fill in for someone as their understudy during an opera. "It was awful actually, due to the circumstances," he said, wiping sweat from his brow. "The lead singer had to jump out a window near the end of the first act. Unfortunately, the mattress he was supposed to land on wasn't in position. Because he'd done the scene so many times, he just jumped. He didn't bother to look and see if the mattress was there to catch him. I still remember hearing the thud as he landed, breaking his leg. I had to rush on stage and take over, of course. The audience had paid good money, and here we were at the beginning of the show.

"To top it all off, I wasn't in costume, I was wearing jeans. I sang my lines while holding the score because I hadn't memorized a thing. After that, I put my nose to the grindstone and learned my part quickly for future performances. To my relief, the scene was changed to have the character crawl out the front door instead of jumping out the window. Talk about a lesson in preparation, or lack of it."

The more stories I heard from the professor, the more I

knew I wanted to be a performer. As a result, I ended up with a bad case of audition fever and tried out for something every weekend.

I knew things were heading in a bad direction when I auditioned for an orange juice commercial and got beaten by a kid with absolutely no experience. I'd definitely hit a dry spell. A slump.

What made things even more frustrating was the fact that Cinnamon wasn't the only one landing gigs. Goldilocks was on a roll. Because of him, some of the other sixth graders had regained their confidence and had started auditioning again. Some of them were now getting parts as well. They didn't go around rubbing it in like Cinnamon did, but I knew I had to keep getting out there, too, if I was going to keep up.

I slouched in the car on the ride home after auditioning for a new diarrhea medicine and getting the boot. "I feel like a loser, a nobody, a total peon."

"No. You no peon," Abuelo said, shaking his head. "You scatter-brained, ditzy. You not the sharpest spoon in the drawer…"

I said peon, not moron!

"Maybe you slow, forgetful, but you not complete—"

"I get the picture, Abuelo!" *How comforting to know I wasn't a* total *moron.*

I kept hoping for possible gigs, so I was really happy when my agent called to tell me out about an open audition for a new children's toothpaste that would be aired nationally. It wasn't going to be aired only locally, like the *Stink-Away* commercial, or statewide like *Jungle Fever*. Nope. We were talking big-time. We were talking about a national audience! The competition would be tough.

When Abuelo and I entered the studio, I not only faced the usual competition of Cinnamon, Tamika, Goldilocks, and some of the other sixth graders, but all kinds of new kids, too.

An assistant handed me a script, and a few minutes later they filed us in one at a time.

Cinnamon sashayed in but stormed out in a huff a minute later. "It's their loss, not mine," she spat out before stomping from the building.

Tamika hustled inside but slunk out just as fast.

Goldilocks went in but never came out.

Kid after kid marched in confidently and slunk back out. Only a few were asked to stay.

Finally, it was my turn. I spotted Goldilocks lounging on a sofa in the back of the room, a tablet in one hand and a soda in the other. The other kids were busy with their cell phones.

I sat up straight, fluffed my hair and read through my lines. "Introducing," I said, holding up a spinach green tube, "Brocco-Brush! A broccoli-flavored toothpaste that tastes delicious and works great! We've added thirty-five different vitamins, so all you have to do is brush with broccoli. You never have to eat it. Yum!" I licked my teeth, as if I had just eaten a scrumptious chocolate bar. "Whenever I use delicious-tasting Brocco-Brush, I just have to smile." I opened the tube, squeezed some onto a brush, grinned, and brushed away.

"Cut!" the director yelled.

That's when I gagged, spitting the green goop all over my red shirt, like I was getting ready for Christmas. *Oops!* But what was I supposed to do with a mouth full of broccoli-flavored mush? Swallow? I bet even Puerquito wouldn't have touched the stuff. Somebody handed me a glass of water. I swigged it down in two seconds flat. Then I remembered I was auditioning for a part. Trying to land a gig. Trying to beat the snootie-patootiness out of Cinnamon Cleaver. "My teeth are a lot whiter, don't you think?" I said to no one in particular.

I tried to make myself hiccup so they would think that's what had caused the eruption all over my blouse. Unfortunately, the 'hiccup' came out sounding like an elephant's burp. The famous words, 'Thanks, but no thanks,' were sure to be uttered soon.

"Thanks, great job," came a voice from the back of the room.

A woman sidled up to me. "Becky Kelsey," she said, shaking my hand. "That was the most convincing one yet. Have a seat." She examined my teeth. "Yes! I think they are a little whiter!"

I watched Goldilocks and the others slink out and then glanced around the empty room. *How did I get the part without having to sing?* It was my crooning that usually put me over the edge.

"We won't shoot the actual commercial for a few weeks," Ms. Kelsey said. "Brocco-Brush hasn't hit the shelves yet, but once it does, we'll give your agent a call. Take care, now."

That's it? Oh, yeah. Here's the part where I'm supposed to get excited. Okay? How come I'm not?

Abuelo asked me about the shoot on the ride home. "Broccoli flavor toothpaste? It taste good?"

I shook my head. "No, it's disgusting. I can't get rid of the rotten taste in my mouth. But it's supposed to have lots of vitamins. So it's good for you."

"Hmm." Abuelo glanced over at me. "But you take job."

"Well...yeah...they offered it to me."

We drove in silence for a few minutes.

I sighed. "I know I should be happy about landing the part and everything, but I don't know...I guess I feel a little... confused. Like something's not quite right."

Abuelo glanced over at me. "You happy you get part, but not happy to sell something not so good?"

I nodded.

Abuelo smiled but didn't say anything.

I tried to smile back but I didn't feel like it.

CHICKEN GOT YOUR TONGUE?

I rushed straight to my room and sprawled out on my bed. *I'll just call my agent and ask her to call the Brocco-Brush people and tell them I can't do the commercial. Easy. I'll call first thing tomorrow. No, the next day. Next week. How about next millennium?*

If I want to get ahead, I should suck it up and just do it. This is a national commercial we're talking about, not some small-time gig. How can I not take this opportunity? Don't endorsements come with being a celebrity? Shouldn't I start now? I wonder if real celebrities ever feel this conflicted?

My frustration over whether or not to do the *Brocco-Brush* commercial got put on hold because after school the next day, we came home to find Abuelo lying on the couch, clutching his stomach and moaning.

Dad rushed over and stood beside him. "What's going on?"

"Don't feel good," Abuelo said.

"Is it the side of your stomach or the middle? If it's the middle it's probably a viral infection. If it's the side, it could be your appendix."

Abuelo kept clutching his stomach. "Hurts everywhere."

My father frowned. "Why don't we head out to the doctor just to be sure?"

"Why?" Abuelo wrinkled his forehead. "The doctor give me medicine. I don't want medicine."

Dad ignored him and helped him out to the car. Rosa and I followed. "Daisy, you stay home with Rosa. I'll call the doctor's office on my cell. They usually leave spots open for emergencies."

I helped Abuelo crawl into the back seat. He seemed uneasy. "Just remember one thing," he said, pulling me close. *This is it,* I thought. *He's giving me his final words of wisdom.* I gulped and clasped his hand. "No matter what the doctor say...," he croaked. "Especially if they send me to hospital for testing." He held his stomach. "Remember..." he muttered, swallowing hard, "sneak me *El Loco Fry Chicken.*"

Abuelo returned a few hours later. No testing. No hospital. He had a mild case of acid indigestion from inhaling too much fried food. He saw Dad putting sprout-covered turkey burgers on the table for dinner and clutched his stomach again.

Even Puerquito ran from the table yelping.

Dad seemed like he was trying to compromise with Abuelo. He started ordering takeout veggie pizza once in a while and served us meatballs made out of real beef— just organic and extra low fat.

Abuelo was trying, too. He started eating yogurt with fruit and granola. And he did it without complaining. He still ate food from *El Loco Fried Chicken*, but only once a week.

I was glad Abuelo and my father had reached a truce in the food department. The downside of a peaceful house was the fact that I had plenty of time to worry about what to do about the upcoming *Brocco-Brush* shoot.

"What's up?" Brad asked at lunch as he drowned his hamburger in ketchup.

"You weren't *this* quiet when you had laryngitis. Chicken got your tongue? Bawk, bawk."

I couldn't believe he was making such a lame joke about my chicken suit. He was probably just trying to get me to talk, but still.

Out of the corner of my eye I saw Tamika watching us. She sat a few tables down with Cinnamon and her gang, mindlessly shoving French fries in her mouth. It didn't seem as if she was listening to what anybody around her was saying. Maybe she would rather have been sitting with Brad and me.

I shot Tamika a hopeful smile. *You could be sitting here, too. And you can if you'd only try and work things out.* She gazed down at the floor and stayed where she was. I took a sip of milk then told Brad what had happened at the *Brocco-Brush* audition. "I want another gig, but I don't know. Something doesn't feel right. It wasn't like they were saying it tasted great, but it only tasted good. This stuff is mega-gross. And I wasn't the only one who thought so."

Brad swallowed a bite of his burger. "That's why I stick to scenery. It's not as complicated. I wish I had the answer for you. All I can say is I don't know how moping around is supposed to help you get into the master class."

"Moping around? Right. I'll call the *Brocco-Brush* people right now and tell them how much I hate their toothpaste. I'm sure they'll recommend me for dozens of other commercials."

Brad hung his head and swung his neck back and forth real fast like a dog trying to shake water off. "Girls..."

"I'm sorry, Brad. I just...."

Right then, I wanted to plop my head in my chili, take a year-long nap, and forget about life, but I didn't think the cafeteria ladies would let me hold the table that long.

I glanced back at Tamika. She was chattering away with Enrique like everything was fine. How I wished she and I were on speaking terms. She had always been such a good listener. It would have been nice if I could have talked to her about the *Brocco-Brush* problem.

———

LATER THAT DAY WE HAD MUSIC CLASS. "IT HAS COME TO MY attention that only a handful of you have had the opportunity to perform before a live audience," said the professor. "Maybe next time we go to the homeless shelter we can do some impromptu performing. This will provide a few souls with needed encouragement and provide some of you with needed performing experience. Miss De La Cruz is also bringing along some clothing donations. Anyone else who would like to contribute is free to do so."

How did he know I was bringing clothes? I'd only mentioned it to Brad, who was also bringing stuff.

"I'd also like to have a cast party after the show. Would anyone like to host it?"

I raised my hand. "We can probably have it at my house. I'll ask my parents."

"Another thing I noticed from serving in the kitchen," said the professor, "is that I've yet to see the residents partake of any sweets. It might be nice if we can provide them with some desserts. My wife is already baking her wonderful shortbread, so please feel free to bring along your favorite dish as well."

It was nice of him to notice the problem about the sweets. Maybe Dad could help me whip up some healthy brownies.

The professor sat at the piano, leading us through all kinds of breathing exercises and vocal arpeggios. Of course, we had to take notes and notate the arpeggios on staff paper so we could practice them on our own later. Then he had us stand in a line to massage each other's backs.

Professor Magoon stood in front of the room. "Today we'll be rehearsing the dances that are part of the musical, so some of the younger students will be joining us. If you are not part of the dance company, you may use this time to review the sheet music for the songs to make sure you've memorized all the words."

A few minutes later, Rosa wandered in with some of the other kids who were dancing in the show. Since Rosa's dance number was first, the professor started the rehearsal with her routine and played the soundtrack.

Rosa stood like a statue and missed her cue.

The professor stopped the music. "You begin your dance two measures in. Since there are four beats in each measure, you'll need to count to four, two times. Got it?"

Rosa nodded. The music started again. "One, two, three, four, one, two, three, four," she shouted to the beat.

Laughter erupted around the room. The professor paused the music and knelt down in front of Rosa. "When we count the beats, we count them in our head or tap our foot along with the music. We don't say anything out loud. Are you ready to try again?"

"Ready, Freddy!" Rosa shouted. When the music started, she swung her hips and tapped her foot along with the beat, but she came in on cue. She remembered every turn, twist and hop then took a bow when she was done.

We all clapped. A moment later, the school secretary wandered in and pulled the professor aside.

Cinnamon used the opportunity to rush up to Rosa and give her a high five. "At least *someone* in the De La Cruz family has talent."

I shook my head and sighed. Rosa had looked adorable up there in her pink leotard and ballet slippers. She deserved the applause. Let Cinnamon be a meanie-pants. I wasn't going to rise to the bait and turn against my own sister. "Way to go, Rosa!" I hollered, pushing my palms toward the ceiling.

"Yeah, good job!" Enrique rushed up to Rosa, grabbed her hand and spun her around. Then the strangest thing happened. Tamika jumped up from her seat, gave Rosa a fist bump and started doing goofy dance moves and jazz hands with her and Enrique. Some of the other kids joined in, too. Everyone was having such a good time, the professor had to flash the lights a few times when he was finished talking, to get our attention and put us back on track.

So much for Cinnamon trying to ruin all the fun.

When Mrs. Sandberg came to lead us back to homeroom after music, I asked her if I could stay behind for a minute to talk to the professor. He seemed to be in a talkative, friendly mood.

As I knocked on his office door I noticed a fresh stack of cluttered sheet music on his desk. I knew what I'd be doing in the morning. "Ah, Miss De La Cruz, I was looking for someone to share some shortbread with." He passed me a plate of cookies. I took one.

"My wife hasn't forgotten how to make a good, old-fashioned, Scottish biscuit."

I bit into it. "These are good. Buttery," I said through a mouth full of crumbs.

"Indeed, they are." He leaned back in his chair. "Now, what can I do for you?"

"Um," I kept munching. "Do you need me to check your box again?"

"I checked it before lunch."

I examined my cookie closely as I munched some more.

"I've got two dozen first-graders descending upon me in…" he checked his gold wristwatch, "three minutes." He put his elbows on his desk and placed the palms of his hands together as if he were about to pray.

I knew I needed to get moving with what I wanted to ask him. I popped the last bite of cookie into my mouth and ran my fingers across the spines of some books on a shelf.

"Have you ever done anything you didn't think was right just to get a gig?"

"Hmm." He made a face like he was thinking. "No, I can't say I have. Why?"

"I, uh, just wondered. That's all."

"I'm not going to say the temptation has never crossed my path. But true talent will rise to the top, in most cases, anyway. And there's a lot to be said for hard work. Cheating, lowering one's standards, not being true to one's sense of right and wrong, all cheapen success. No... I'd rather make my way honestly. Then I also earn respect. From myself, as well as others." He stood up. "There you have my take on it."

I heard the pitter patter of first-grade feet. "Thanks. That gives me something to think... I mean... you know... wonder about." And I did think about it. All afternoon.

FRIED MUSKRAT

A few days later, we went on another afterschool field trip to the homeless shelter.

Two policemen stood waiting for us again when we arrived. As we took our seats, I spotted some of the same people from our last visit. But there was someone different this time. A boy, about my age, sat alone in a corner on a window ledge. I wondered why he wasn't in school until I noticed his jeans and T-shirt were filthy. I couldn't help but feel for him. *He wouldn't last a minute at our school. Somebody would eat him for lunch before he even made it to lunch.*

The professor didn't waste any time getting started. He stood on the stage and asked the audience for song requests.

A woman holding a toddler called out, "My little Sammy wants to hear *Sweeter Than Brown Sugar.*"

The professor scanned the room. "A great classic. Anyone know it?"

"I do," Enrique called out. He was totally into retro music and was hoping to make his mark singing covers of classic songs.

"You're on," the professor said, sitting down at the piano.

Enrique strolled onto the stage, belting out the tune.

"Sweeter than brown sugar is my love to me. Sweeter than the honey coming from the bee...."

Several of the residents sang along with him. He strolled over to a woman sitting with a colorful quilt on her lap and handed her the microphone.

The woman croaked along. "Sweeter than molasses, cotton candy, too. For my love is tender, and my love is true."

Enrique strutted over to several others who sang along with him. That was one thing I liked about Enrique. He didn't hog the stage, but included others. He just wanted everyone to have a good time. It wasn't like he always had to be top dog and have all the attention focused on him. It was nice that someone like him had gotten a solo in the school musical, even if he did tease people sometimes.

When he finished, the residents clapped like they had just watched a famous entertainer performing.

The professor stood before the crowd. "Anything else you'd like to hear?"

A tall man with shoulder-length, white hair spoke up. "I thought you had dancers? I've got some tunes from the roaring twenties." He held up a CD. "You got anyone who can keep up with this?"

The professor glanced around. "Okay, dancers. Who's up to the task?"

Cinnamon didn't bother to raise her hand. She hopped from her seat, grabbed the CD, and examined the song titles. "Let's do number three."

Cinnamon danced the Charleston as music rang out from the professor's portable sound system. Her knee slapping, toe tapping, and arm flapping were so accurate, it seemed as if she'd grown up dancing the Charleston. The only thing she lacked was the flapper costume the dancers used to wear. It was actually fun watching her, considering it was meanie-pants Cinnamon.

The man who requested the dance number stood up and joined her. He didn't just keep up with her roaring 1920's style, but threw in some moves from the 1960s like the Funky Chicken and the Swim. The audience went wild when Cinnamon and the man finished.

Cinnamon actually let someone share the spotlight with her? That's a first.

An elderly woman leaning on a cane spoke up. "Let's have some more singing. Does anyone know *Forever, Valentine*? That was always one of my favorites."

"Does anyone know *Forever, Valentine*?" Professor Magoon repeated, glancing around the room. As his gaze landed on me, he nodded a little, like he was trying hard to forget my unforgettable audition. "Uh, maybe I can plunk it out on the keyboard," he stammered.

"Oh, I'd much rather hear singing than plunking," the woman said.

"Me too," came another voice from the crowd.

"Daisy knows it by heart," Brad hollered out.

I kept quiet. It would be crazy to act too eager after the lousy, and only, performance the professor had ever seen me do.

Professor Magoon stared into the audience, wringing his hands. He was probably just trying to save me from embarrassing myself. I wasn't exactly chomping at the bit to try it again either. The song had already been destroyed once by me already. It was probably jinxed. I'd never be able to sing it right ever again. *Nope. There are plenty of other songs. I'll wait until they ask for one I'm sure I can do.*

Just then, Cinnamon turned around in her seat, sending me one of her nasty scowls. I felt myself getting hot and it wasn't because of the temperature. *You are sooo not going to have the last* word, *Cinnamon Cleaver*. *Not today. Not ever.* I stood up and marched over to the professor. "I can do it."

"Are you sure you're up to it?" he whispered.

"We're in a homeless shelter. Singing for free. Who will it hurt?" I whispered back.

"My ears" is what I thought he might say, but instead he whispered, "I suppose we can cut it short if we have to."

He sat down at the keyboard and played the introduction.

I stood tall with my back straight and my feet a few inches apart, bending my knees slightly like the professor had taught us. I inhaled deeply using my diaphragm and belted out the words. "Forever, Valentiiiiiine! Forever, Valentiiiiiiiine! I'll love you truly, truly, Valentiiiiiiiine. We'll always be together, Valentii-iiiiine. In winter, spring, and summer, Valentiiiiiiiiiine, for you will be forever miiiiiiiiiiine." I sang as if I were performing at the White House for the President and his honored guests.

Several members of the audience snapped, or clapped along with the beat. Professor Magoon and most of my class looked as if they had just seen a dead cat resurrected to another of its nine lives. Cinnamon and Tamika wore the only unhappy faces in the crowd.

I sang out strongly through the rest of the song. Whoops and hollers rang out from the audience when it ended.

I did it! I sang it with no mistakes!

The show kept going, and a few other kids sang or danced. I was surprised Tamika didn't jump up and strut her stuff when someone requested a popular gospel duet. When the professor asked for volunteers she slid down in her seat like she was trying to hide. *All this pushing and shoving to get ahead and now she's chickening out?* Enrique ended up singing it with one of the women from the shelter.

As usual, the professor asked for volunteers to serve in the lunch line. As amazing as it seemed, everyone volunteered, even

Cinnamon. It made me wonder if Brad had asked everyone to help ahead of time. Or maybe he'd told them it wasn't so bad. Maybe people felt more comfortable helping this time because they'd gotten involved and brought something for dessert. Or maybe they were just getting used to the place. Whatever the reason for the change, it was encouraging to see people wanting to help.

As the policemen led us all to the cafeteria, we filed past the same rickety furniture we'd seen the last two times we were there.

"I didn't know people actually lived like this," Cinnamon said to Tamika.

When we reached the kitchen area, the staff members put some of us to work dishing up plates of rice and beans. The rest of us got busy serving the desserts we'd brought. Tamika and I ended up standing side-by-side placing brownie slices onto small paper plates. Our shoulders accidentally touched, but she didn't seem to notice. It was just like old times except that we were quiet.

Maybe she's starting to feel comfortable around me again. Maybe she misses me as much as I miss her.

No one spoke much. The usual teasing and competitiveness was, for once, nowhere to be found. It was as if a winged fairy had floated in, waved her magic wand, and cast a spell over all of us saying, "You will forget all your cares and worries when I show you what real trouble is."

Once we'd cleaned up the kitchen and the members of the shelter had eaten lunch, the professor had us show them the donations we'd brought. I found some of the older women and gave them some of the housedresses my next-door neighbor, Mrs. Miller, had given me. She'd gotten so many clothing presents from her children, she hadn't had a chance to wear them all. Some of the dresses still had tags on them.

The woman who had requested *Forever, Valentine* spoke up. "God has given you quite a gift, young lady. I hope you'll continue to use it to make people happy. What a nice present you've given to us. Thank you so much." I wasn't sure if she was talking about my singing or the fact that I'd brought her some clothes. But it didn't matter. I'd brought a smile to someone's face.

"You're welcome. My name's Daisy, by the way."

The woman beamed. "My name's Hadassah, but most people call me Miss Haddie. We enjoyed having you visit with us. You're welcome here anytime."

It was nice to see someone being so grateful for such a small gift. "Thanks. I'll remember that."

I greeted some of the other women. They seemed a little shy about coming up to us, but their children weren't. The professor, along with Brad, had managed to come up with some toys for the children. The kids ran around showing everyone what they got. They jumped up and down acting like it was Christmas or Hanukkah.

One little girl ran around giving away hugs and drawings she had colored. She handed me a picture of a house with a great big sun. How many times had I drawn scenes like that myself when I was younger? I hadn't stopped to think that living in your own home wasn't an automatic part of life for everyone, even if your house was an old fixer-upper like mine.

The children, as well as the adults, devoured the desserts we'd brought. The staff members had told us we could have some, too, but not one student from our school touched anything. Everyone seemed to know, instinctively, that we could eat what we wanted whenever we wanted to and that this was a real treat for them. One that was probably rare.

On the way out, someone picked up a stray sneaker. It was brand new, with the sticker still attached, so it had obviously come from a donation bag. The professor was about to put it back in his paper sack, but one of the women asked him for it. "That'll fit my Sammy. He lost his left shoe, but now he can use this one." I glanced around at everyone else. We all seemed to be in shock that someone was so desperate for shoes they'd purposely let their child wear a pair that didn't match.

Most of the donations had been brought over in paper bags. Some of the prettier bags were from nice stores at the mall. As Brad, a few other students, and I collected the bags, some of the women asked us for them. A couple of the women snatched at the bags, trying to get at them before anyone else did. We tried to be fair and give everyone who wanted some at least two.

It was amazing to see people get excited over being given a bag that most of us would have thrown away or recycled. As yet, I'd never seen that type of poverty and I had a hunch no one else in my class had either.

It was quieter than usual on the bus ride back to school. We had all packed bag lunches, which we were supposed to wolf down on the way back. I nibbled at my apple, but it was hard to eat. Brad sat next to me, and even though he could gorge himself in the middle of a hurricane warning, he was having trouble finishing his turkey and cheese on rye.

Lots of kids hung their heads or stared out the windows with tears in their eyes. One girl was out and out crying. The professor had planned ahead and passed a few tissue boxes around.

I scanned the bus for Tamika. When I spotted her, she was already watching me. She looked like she had just come from a funeral parlor instead of a homeless shelter. We both glanced away after a few seconds.

Cinnamon sat next to her. I caught Cinnamon's eye, but not on purpose. I waited for her to throw a scowl my way, but none came. *Do I detect a tear? Yup, her eyes are definitely red.*

She went back to examining the picture the girl at the shelter had given her. *Finally. No more backbiting, meanness, or dirty looks.*

I felt a tap on my shoulder after I climbed off the bus. It was the professor. He had a serious look on his face. "I want to talk. Meet me in the music room."

Brad and I glanced at each other but didn't dare say anything.

I headed back inside the school building and headed straight to the professor's office, wondering what he wanted. Maybe he was angry with me about something I'd just done or he needed help with some kind of urgent task.

When I walked in, he was sitting at his desk. He got right to the point. "I'd like you to understudy the lead singing role in *La Isla Del Encanto.* I wasn't going to bother with understudies, but I've changed my mind."

I stood in front of his desk not knowing what to say.

"I don't need your answer right now. Take a few days to think it over. Then get back to me on it, will you?" He grabbed his plan book and started writing.

Brad stood waiting for me when I strode out. "So? What did old Magoon want?"

I had a hard time holding back a grin as we headed toward homeroom. "Oh, he was wondering when the temperature would dip below 9000 degrees. And he needed some good recipes for fried muskrat and poached 'possum. He's having a party."

Brad placed the back of his hand against his forehead, pretending to swoon like one of those frilly dressed women in an old-time movie. "I must know or I'll die."

I laughed as we reached the outdoor breezeway. "Okay, okay. He asked me to think about understudying lead vocals for *La Isla Del Encanto.*"

Brad beamed. "He must have been totally blown away when he heard you sing. You told him you'd do it, right?"

I stopped at the water fountain for a drink. "He told me to think about it, so that's what I'm going to do. I'd have to learn a big part I probably won't even get to sing. That's a lot of work. It might not be worth all the trouble." I wiped my mouth.

"Hey, now you and Tamika will *have* to start talking again. How can you keep going with this not-speaking-to-each-other-business when you've both got to learn the same part? Nah! Ya'll got to get yourselves back together." He held his hand up for a fist bump.

I crossed my arms and stared at him. "Brad..."

Brad raised his eyebrows and walked two feet in front of me, pretending to be mad. "Fine. Don't understudy," he said. "That sounds like way too much work. You'd be better off sticking to frying muskrats and poaching 'possums." He headed toward the carpool line.

I followed behind, thinking about whether I wanted to understudy or not. I'd be understudying for Tamika. She would probably rub it in. If she didn't, Cinnamon sure would. On the other hand, it was a definite promotion from the chorus. It was almost like the professor was giving me a sign of approval. He must have thought I had at least some sort of talent as a vocalist to offer me the part. Unless he was worried about Tamika, since she'd hung back today and hadn't volunteered to sing anything.

Part of me felt happy that I'd been asked, but it was hard to feel too excited after visiting a homeless shelter. For some reason my mind kept drifting to the dirty boy we'd seen. I wondered how he'd react if I told him about my problems.

Please help me, kid. This is life or death. I can't decide whether or not to understudy for a role at school. Oh, and also, I can't figure out whether to shoot a national commercial that promotes a lousy product.

How would he feel if I told him my big dream was to make it in show business someday? What if we compared dreams? What if he told me his big dream was to have some new clothes? Or to get out of the shelter and into a real home? Or to be part of a loving family? I had all those things. But did I really appreciate them?

I knew I couldn't have my eyes opened to seeing people in need and then pretend those kinds of problems didn't exist. Whatever my dreams or plans were, I didn't want to be that kind of person. I decided that while I'd still keep my old dreams, I'd make room for some new ones, too. New dreams that included finding ways to help other people.

FULL OF VIPERS

Abuelo came to church with us on Sunday. "I haven't taken come onion in a few weeks," he said, on the ride over.

"Come onion?" I asked.

"Nope. No onions at church," said Rosa. "Unless you want an onion bagel beforehand, but you have to get there early."

"No. How you say?" Abuelo squinted. "Take the Lord's zipper?"

"Ah." I giggled. "The Lord's supper. Yes. You can take communion at church."

No one said anything after that, but a few snorts and chortles escaped from my parents who were sitting in the front seat.

Once we got to church, I wandered off to my pre-teen class, like I usually did. Our youth pastor asked us to turn to Luke chapter six. "In verse thirty-one, the Bible tells us that we should treat others the same way we would like to be treated. It's not about just having good intentions. It's about actually doing something about the needs of our friends, families, and the people around us."

Wow. I spent a lot of time worrying about my own problems,

without giving much thought to what was going on with other people. That verse sure gave me a lot to think about.

———

"WHY DON'T WE TAKE A PICNIC LUNCH OUT TO THE BEACH?" DAD asked when we got home. "We have to eat, anyway. We may as well go somewhere with a good view."

Even though it wasn't summertime anymore, it was still fairly hot in Miami, so we all got changed, helped pack up fruit, sandwiches, and water bottles, and headed off to the ocean.

When we got there, Rosa and I built sandcastles and looked for seashells. Black was my favorite color to find because most of them seemed to be either white or orange.

Once we each collected a handful, Abuelo let us bury him in the sand. When it was time to leave, he pretended to be asleep and wouldn't get up, even after we'd packed up all our stuff and wandered off a few yards toward the parking lot.

"I don't feel like cooking dinner," Mom said. "You guys want to go through the *El Loco Fried Chicken* drive-thru on the way home?"

Abuelo shot up out of the sand. "I drive home, if you want, J.R."

Dad smirked. "You don't trust me to take everyone to the drive-thru?"

Abuelo shook his head and held out his hand for the keys. "I drive." And he drove to the restaurant like he was competing in a race.

———

ON MONDAY MORNING, BRAD HANDED ME A BOOK WHILE I WAS sitting in the library.

I read the title. *Gloria Florez: Up Close and in Person.* "How'd you know I like her?"

He smirked.

A bookmark had been placed in the chapter titled *Auditions.* I skimmed through it. "Listen to this," I said. "G-Flo auditioned fourteen times before getting a lead role. She used to understudy all the time and got some parts because she could perform them on short notice." I closed the book slowly.

"Don't forget to ask Tamika if she'll start practicing with you again," Brad said as he logged onto a nearby computer.

I raised my eyebrows.

"Just ask her, okay?" He sure was persistent.

———

I WENT TO PROFESSOR MAGOON'S OFFICE AT DISMISSAL TIME AND told him I would understudy.

"Wise choice," he said, handing me the musical score and CD.

As soon as I got home I started learning my part. Visiting the shelter had helped me to not feel so much pressure about making it into the master class. I wanted to learn and I wanted to do my best, but it didn't seem like my world was going to fall apart if I didn't make it in. I'd have other chances to learn and grow. *Haven't I learned a lot from the professor already?*

What I needed to do about the *Brocco-Brush* commercial had also become clear. But did I have the guts to do it? I spoke to Mom about it one night after dinner as I was helping with the dishes.

"A lot of people think running a library is all about shelving books and keeping track of fines, but there's a lot more to it than that," she said, rinsing off a plate. "I have to make tough decisions sometimes. I think hard about my choices because what I decide will affect a lot of people."

It didn't seem like my decision would affect other people, at first. But when I thought about it, I realized if I went on television and said *Brocco-Brush* was great, some people might actually buy it. And they'd be wasting their money. No one would ever use it after putting it in their mouth unless they didn't have any taste buds.

I went upstairs, sat down on my bed, and went over my notes from the sermon I'd heard on Sunday. Our pastor had showed us a verse that said we should treat others the same way we want to be treated.

I kneeled next to my bed and prayed for guidance. Then I thought everything through again.

My agent had emailed to tell me Ms. Kelsey would be contacting me, but she hadn't called to set up the shoot, and if I didn't reach her in time, I'd be stuck doing the commercial. It wouldn't exactly be considerate if they had to search for someone else at the last minute.

I'd figured out that there were worse things than not getting a gig or ending up in the master class, more than one way to follow my heart and reach my goals. *I may not know how I am going to reach my goals, but I know how I'm not going to reach them.*

I grabbed the phone, dialed the number on the business card, and waited.

"Daytona Discoveries," a woman's voice said.

"Um, can I talk to someone about the *Brocco-Brush* commercial I'm supposed to shoot?"

"Daisy? Is that you? It's Becky. Talk to me, honey."

I took a deep breath. "Well, I, uh...I'm sure the toothpaste is great and everything, but the problem is...it didn't taste good to me. So...I don't think I'm the best person to promote it." *There. I said it. It was out. Phew!*

"Oh, sugar, don't worry your pretty little head. To tell you the truth, we've had trouble getting it on the shelves. Not too many stores want to carry it. There's no use spending all that money airing a commercial for something people can't or won't buy. So...it's on hold for now. I was just sitting here working late, thinking about what to do. I'm sorry I didn't contact you sooner. I guess I was in a little bit of denial."

"I'm sorry it's not working out for you," I said. "But thanks for understanding."

"No problem, sweet pea. You take care, you hear."

It was amazing how one little phone call could make me feel so much lighter. I'd been walking around feeling like I was carrying a piano on my back, when the problem had been out of my hands all along.

It was also amazing how within a few short days of going to the shelter everyone at school had slipped right back into acting the way they always had before the trip.

I sat in music class the day before the performance of *La Isla Del Encanto*. Things were still rough between Tamika and me. Brad had given up on us ever being friends again and had started sitting with some of the boys.

He had phoned me the night before. "Tamika keeps chewing me out because I have the nerve to still hang out with you," he'd said. "Nothing personal, but she's got a big mouth, and I gotta keep the peace."

I knew he was telling the truth. He was too good of a friend to lie to me. Even someone as easy-going as Brad had his limits when it came to dealing with difficult people, even if that difficult person happened to be his own sister. Which left me stuck sitting next to the biggest wisecracks in the sixth grade, Enrique and Manuel.

"Do you have any old clothes you don't wear anymore?" I asked them. "Like for a kid your age?"

"What do you want with boy's clothes?" Enrique asked. "Don't tell me you're so desperate for a gig you're starting to audition for male roles."

Manuel guffawed. "What are you auditioning for? The latest he-man deodorant? Like guys are gonna buy a deodorant *you're* trying to sell!"

"Hey, they might," Enrique said, "If she dressed up as a giant can of it!"

They sat there, laughing their guts out.

I crossed my arms and sighed. "They're not for me."

"Then who are they for? Brad?" Manuel said. "I noticed you're not so chummy with him anymore. What'd you do? Steal a role from him?"

"Yeah, and now she needs to bring him a peace offering," said Enrique.

I clicked my tongue. "For your information, I want to give them to that kid we saw at the homeless shelter."

"No way," Manuel said. "I'm not giving up anything of mine."

Enrique nodded. "I got extra clothes, Dais. I'll bring you some stuff."

The professor finally came out of his office and had us stand for our vocal warm-up exercises. "Miss De La Cruz, will you take us through our routine?"

Wow! So far, he hasn't asked anyone to help him with this kind of stuff.

"Oh, sure." I strolled up to the front of the room. "Um, okay, everyone stand with your backs against the wall and bend your knees so your back stays flat. Breathe in slowly, using your diaphragm, for four counts. Then exhale slowly for eight counts. When you exhale pretend your midsection is a tire with a slow leak and hiss slowly like this, *sssssss.* Ready?"

Everyone breathed in for four counts and then exhaled for eight. It sounded like the room was full of vipers. In a way, it was.

As I glanced around the room, I didn't see anyone who was on my side.

The professor took over. "Okay, on this next exercise, make sure your lips vibrate on the M sound, like this." He sang, "Me, may, ma, moe, moo, me, may, ma, moe, moo," on the same note. He had us repeat after him, raising the starting note a half step each time we sang the pattern.

We clasped our hands in front of our waists and twisted from side to side, exhaling with each twist. This was supposed to send clean, fresh air into our lungs so we'd sound better. We blew raspberries with our lips and slid up and down scales singing arpeggios on all kinds of nonsense syllables.

After taking us through our vocal exercises, the professor paced the room. "The performance of the musical is tomorrow. So this is it, the last mile at the end of a long marathon. I expect any shortcomings we've experienced during rehearsals to be cleared up by tomorrow. And, Miss De La Cruz, I take it the cast party is in place?" the professor asked me.

I nodded. I'd offered to host the party since Dad had finished painting. While all the updates on our house still weren't finished yet, it looked good enough for now.

The professor scanned the room. "One more thing. The list of the students invited to join the master class will be posted on Monday morning. Is there anything else we need to be aware of?" It seemed like no one breathed once he reminded us of the master class. "Alright then. Let's file into the auditorium and take it from the top."

I stayed near the back of the line and waited for everyone else to go in. Tamika hung back also. She turned around and glanced at me a few times like she was about to say something, but she never spoke a word.

After rehearsal, I followed the professor to his office.

"What can I do for you?" he asked, taking a seat behind his desk.

"It might be nice if we sent an invitation to the shelter so people can come and see the show."

"Wonderful idea." The professor nodded. "In fact, it's such a good idea, it's already been taken care of."

"It has?"

"I've got a keen interest in the homeless, as I used to be homeless myself."

"You were?" I couldn't think of anything else to say.

The professor straightened a few books on his desk. "When I first got out of college the only work I could get was ushering at the theatre. In my spare time I watched the shows, desperate to learn whatever I could. My income wasn't enough to buy food *and* pay rent. Not in London, anyway. I'd sleep in a chair or the corner of a dressing room. I always managed to sleep indoors, except for the first time I went on stage as an understudy. After the show, I was so befuddled I left the theatre with everyone else and got locked out. I ended up sleeping *behind* the theater in the alley. That was an experience, I tell you. So...the homeless will always hold a special place in my heart."

I couldn't believe someone who ended up becoming so successful had gone through such a hard time when he was starting out.

"When did you finally get a place to live?"

"After obtaining the role I was understudying for, I earned enough to rent a small place. My landlord had a beautiful daughter, who I ended up marrying. So you see, it all worked out for the best."

I stood frozen to my spot. *Talk about a colorful life. Making it in the entertainment industry is hard work, that's for sure.*

The professor opened his plan book. "Anything else?"

I figured since he was giving me the chance to ask a question, I'd go ahead and ask one. "Why did you decide to come here after all the great things you've done?"

"One, payback. I've had lots of help along the way. Now it's time for me to help others. Two, careers don't last forever. My voice has been shot for some time now."

No way! Your voice goes on vacation? Permanently? It doesn't last? "But your singing is so powerful. I love hearing you do the warm ups. I wish you'd perform an aria for us."

"Well, thank you. Maybe I will sing for you all sometime." The professor offered me a piece of shortbread. I declined the cookie, but left with a lot to think about.

DODGING A COCONUT

At six o'clock the next evening, I peered out from behind the velvety black drapes on stage. I wore the same outfit as the rest of the female members of the chorus: a white headscarf, white ruffled blouse, and red peasant skirt. The show was scheduled to start at seven, but lots of people were already seated. A large crowd was expected and people from the homeless shelter began arriving.

My family and some of the other neighbors had all cleaned out our closets and donated clothing. A few of the men wore plaid shirts, ties, or jackets, so the professor had probably cleaned out his closet as well.

Someone was calling my name, so I let go of the curtains.

"Daisy, can we talk?" I turned to see Tamika. *Tamika wants to talk to me?* She wasn't in costume, and her hair looked like she hadn't combed it in days. "Now," she added, sounding desperate.

She meandered past the stage, down a back staircase, and led me to a dressing room in the far corner of the basement known as 'the dungeon.'

I glanced around warily. The room was cluttered with costumes hanging from hooks on the walls. *Is Cinnamon hiding somewhere ready to douse me with water? Are they going to lock me in 'the dungeon' so I can't even perform in the chorus?* I planted myself in the doorway, in case they *were* plotting something, but there was no sign of Cinnamon.

"Okay, what's this all about?" I asked her. "The show is starting soon."

Tamika burst into tears. "I can't go out there!"

Here come the stage-fright shenanigans, just like in third grade.

"Why not?"

"I'm scared to death!" she almost screamed.

I smirked and crossed my arms. "Yeah, right. You shot the Miss Drumstix commercial. You were on TV."

"Yeah, but you and Cinnamon were with me." She wiped her tears. "And there wasn't a crowd, just a few stagehands. Have you seen how many people are out there?"

I shrugged. "A lot. Same as usual."

Tamika started howling again. "And what about all the people the professor invited? Like his nephew from ETV. They're all supposed to come."

"Okay, so? We've known about this for months. What do you want me to do?"

"Do the show!" She banged her fists against a big brown lump sitting on a table nearby. "You know the part."

"What's that?" I pointed to the big brown blob.

"A coconut suit. It wasn't ready until today. You won't have to wear it until the final act."

No way. Not another dorky costume.

"Oh, no you don't. I am soooo not wearing that. Not today, not ever."

She pounded the coconut. "You have to. You owe me."

My mouth opened in shock. "Owe you?"

Owe you what, a T-shirt that says 'traitor'?

"We've been friends a long time." She started bawling again.

"I thought we were friends!"

"You were the one who quit calling and cozied up to Miss Big Hair!" I groaned and took a seat on a nearby stool.

She gazed at me with tear-stained eyes. "I'm sorry, Daisy. I miss you. You're right. Cinnamon is a total big-haired-bragging-pain-in-the-neck."

Did she mean it?

I sighed. "Wow. I'm glad you've finally woken up. But, hello! Earth to Tamika! You have to get dressed! The show is about to start!" I could feel tears bubbling up, so I turned to leave.

Tamika had a look of panic in her eyes that said she might pick me up and put me on the stage herself. "You gotta go on. You wanted the role." She shoved the coconut suit at me.

I threw it right back. "I told you. I am *not* wearing this."

"You have to help me!" she said, grabbing hold of my clothes.

I fell back onto the stool and hung my head. *It would be so easy to take the lead from Tamika right now, especially when I know I can nail it. With or without having to wear that stupid coconut suit, it'll put me in a much better position to make it into the master class. Then...who knows what will happen?*

I thought about the day Abuelo arrived unexpectedly and Tamika was eager to help me clean up the house. And at the nursing home a few years back, she'd let me sing a few lines of her precious solo. I was learning that good friends couldn't be replaced so easily.

I was also learning that I couldn't just *say* the right thing. I needed to *do* the right thing. That cleared up all the confusion about what to do.

"Get dressed," I told her.

"Me?" Tamika froze. "But you know the part!"

"So do you." I grabbed the dress she was supposed to wear in her opening number and pushed it toward her. "You can do this. You *wanted* to do it, remember? If you're going to be a performer, you have to get over this stage fright business. If you don't get over it now, when will you?"

She stared back at me, unmoving. It was clear she was thinking it over. "Can you get my mom, just in case?"

I crossed my arms. "There's no time. And anyway, if you have a way out, you'll take it. You only have to say a few lines and sing one short song in the first half. The girls in the chorus will be on stage standing right next to you. Your big solo isn't until the end and then *everyone* will be on stage right along with you. I'll be near the stage the whole time, and Brad will be close by doing the lighting. You'll be fine."

She still hadn't put her dress on, so I grabbed her bandana and started tying it around her head.

"I don't know," she said, her voice quivering.

I took hold of her shoulders and glanced up at her. "The first minute will be tough. But if you can get through that, the rest of the show will feel just like rehearsal. I promise."

She started putting on the dress. I tried to keep talking to distract her. "Rosa is the one with the tough job. She's up first and she's never done a solo before. I haven't heard one complaint from her." *Of course, that's because she's a natural born ham and she loves attention.* "So if she can do it...."

Somehow we made it up the stairs in time for roll call. Tamika latched on to me the way a frightened toddler clings to its mother.

Cinnamon caught sight of us standing together but glanced away and ignored us. The curtains opened as we watched from the wings.

"I'll be right back," Tamika said, rushing off.

Professor Magoon raised his baton, and the orchestra began to play.

"Oohs" and "Ahs" burst from the audience as Rosa tiptoed onto the stage wearing her miniature Bomba dancer outfit. She began her knee bends, toe taps, and endless twirls. She did one too many, teetered sideways and fell over. As the music wound down, she dusted herself off, bustled to the front edge of the stage and called out in a loud voice. "It's okay that I messed up. I'm only doing this for fun. I want to be a vegetarian when I grow up and help puppies deliver their babies." Then she skipped off the stage.

I started laughing. I couldn't help it. Only Rosa would call attention to the fact she'd made a mistake and then blow it off like it was nothing.

Cinnamon got into position to make her entrance. She glided on stage gracefully wearing fluffy pantaloons beneath a flowing white dress. She began the *Bomba* dance as the drumbeat started, but a moment later she wore a frown and moved stiffly.

When Rosa left the stage, the lights had been dimmed. They should have been changed to blue upon Cinnamon's entrance. Instead, different colored lights came on briefly and then flickered off, leaving the stage in total darkness in between colors.

I rushed over to the lighting booth. There was no sign of Brad. Instead, Manuel, who was in charge of the scenery, sat in his place.

"What's going on?" I whispered.

"Tamika started freaking out. Brad is downstairs dealing with her."

"What? Not again! I thought she was just going to the girls' room." I headed toward the stairs to find them.

"You can't leave, too. You're going on soon. Let Brad deal with her," Manuel said as his fingers raced across a row of buttons. He pressed a few. All the stage lights came on, as well as the lights in the audience. Sweat dripped down his forehead. He pushed another button. As he did, huge fans blasted air from the far corner of the stage, right at Cinnamon.

She tried using the swishing movements of the *Bomba* dance to keep her dress down, but it was no use. The fans blew the flounces of her gown up and over her head.

I stole a glance at Professor Magoon. He conducted the music with stiff arms and had a look on his face that said, "Help!"

Cinnamon's scarf flew off, and her hair blew around over the top of her dress. At least her hairpiece hadn't flown off and hit somebody in the face.

Cinnamon wouldn't help me if I accidentally swam into a swamp full of alligators, but I couldn't stand by and watch the professor suffer. A lot of other people had worked hard on the show, too. I had to do something. I'd never done lighting before, but I'd been on stage in the chorus for countless shows and had seen what the lighting crew had done. I caught sight of a huge lever, separate from the others, with a switch going from side to side. I tiptoed behind Manuel and whispered, "If you push this over to the right the fans should shut off." He pushed it and the fans slowed down.

I took a deep breath, scanning the control panel. I located a large black lever I thought would dim the houselights. It worked. The audience lights dimmed as soon as I pushed it.

Our fingers raced over the rest of the switches searching for the buttons that would turn the stage lights to blue. We tried pressing several different buttons. Purple lights flickered on, then green, then yellow. Manuel tried one more button and the lights finally changed to blue. He found the spotlight, shining it on Cinnamon. By the time we'd gotten things under control, her dance number was almost over.

Manuel sighed, leaning back in his chair. "Thanks for your help!" he whispered.

The audience started clapping and then there were all kinds of rumblings.

"Poor thing."

"I don't believe it."

"She's usually such a good dancer."

As I was heading back, a flustered parent volunteer made his way toward the sound and lighting booth. Cinnamon trailed behind the man, fuming.

He lumbered up to Manuel. "What's going on? I'm trying to keep the little kids under control. I can't be everywhere at once!"

Manuel gazed at him sheepishly and filled him in. "I think I'll be okay if we stick to the spotlight and the dimmer. Nothing fancy."

The parent didn't seem convinced. "Are you sure?"

"I'm sure," Manuel said.

The man visibly relaxed as Brad and Tamika wandered up.

"Are you alright?" I asked her.

She nodded. "I did some deep breathing exercises and I'm feeling a lot better."

"Okay, good," said the parent volunteer. "I'll give the professor the thumbs up. He's sweating like crazy out there." Then he hurried away.

Cinnamon shot her Ice Queen glare at me before storming off to the green room.

I followed her. She was guzzling a bottle of water, but she put her bottle down with a bang when she spotted me. "Cinnamon, what happened was—"

"All your fault. I knew you were ambitious," she spat. "But I can't believe you're such a back-stabber. You totally ruined my dance. Don't think I won't get you for this."

"But it *wasn't* my fault. I was the one who got things under—"

She stormed out, letting the door slam behind her.

How can Cinnamon call me a back-stabber? I have my weaknesses like everybody else, but give me a break. I've never been the one to pick a fight with her. She's the one always picking fights with me.

Manuel found me and led me back to where Tamika and the rest of the chorus stood waiting in the wings. "You're up next, guys."

Great, just great. I'm supposed to be helping Tamika and I don't feel like going on myself. Nothing like a heavy dose of Cinnamon to suck all the joy and confidence from a person.

The introduction to the fast-paced song started. Plodding forward like a zombie, I glanced behind to make sure Tamika was following me. I grabbed a pair of maracas from a shelf and followed the red dots of tape to my spot on the stage while Tamika found her spot center stage. A sea of eyes watched, so I breathed deeply as I faced the audience. I forced a smile and shot it Tamika's way. She shot one right back, so I knew she was okay. "*La Isla Del Encanto,*" she sang.

"It's my homeland, it's my homeland," the members of the chorus chimed in, while shaking our maracas from side to side.

"*La Isla Del Encanto*, is known as Puerto Rico." Tamika needed to sing louder and stronger, but at least she was still on stage and not dangling from the edge ready to jump off.

She missed her next entrance and came in late but she sped up her words and caught up with the beat of the orchestra. Most people probably didn't even notice.

We all sang in unison at the end of the song. I took a deep breath and sang, '*La Isla Del Encanto,*' nailing the high A and singing it extra loud because I knew most of the girls, including Tamika, couldn't hit it. We left the stage as the audience clapped.

Tamika held her chest, taking several deep breaths, once we were back stage. "I did it. I actually did it."

"And you can do it again." I nodded, breathing heavily myself. "Time to get downstairs and change for your next number."

She headed down the stairs then turned back to me. "Thanks, Dais."

Cinnamon had another dance solo and headed toward the stage. As she raced past me I noticed the back of her skirt. It was tucked into her tights. In her hurry to change she probably hadn't bothered to check herself in the mirror.

Professor Magoon didn't need any more accidents. I pointed. "Cinnamon!"

She glanced down at her outfit but didn't seem to understand. I raced over, tugging her skirt free as the music began.

Cinnamon danced on stage to applause. The audience obviously felt bad for her after the lighting glitches she'd faced earlier.

I hope she'll finally realize I didn't ruin her dance.

At intermission I was thirsty, so I wandered to the green room for some water. I strolled in as Brad entered from the other direction.

He poured himself some water. "You okay?"

I rolled my eyes. "Except for getting exposed to too much Cinnamon."

Brad sighed. "I wouldn't take it personally. Her mother's out of town again, and I don't think she's seen her father all year. Her housekeeper's the only one who came to see the show. That's got to be tough."

"Yeah." His words explained a lot, even though her meanness hurt. "I better go see what's going on. Tamika can't miss her cue."

Brad punched me playfully on the shoulder. "Thanks for taking care of my sister."

The rest of the show was like riding an airboat through the Everglades: loud and smooth. The air tingled with excitement, and lots of kids were hugging or giving high-fives and fist bumps to each other as they left the stage.

When Cinnamon realized I had prevented her from being embarrassed again, she didn't turn friendly toward me, but at least she stopped throwing dirty looks and accusations my way.

I camped out in the wings and watched Tamika get through her speaking lines with no mistakes then changed into my costume for the final number.

After everyone lined up for the finale, Professor Magoon raised his baton in the air and spicy Latin music rang out from the orchestra.

The curtains opened to a set designed to look like an outdoor feast. The dancers wore leotards of red, yellow, or gold and held matching streamers that swirled, flame-like, as they danced.

The chorus waddled onto stage, standing amidst the 'flames', dressed as pork roasts, drumsticks, beans, plantains, and other food items. I was dressed as a pineapple, so at least I was in yellow, which was a pretty color. I was so glad I had escaped the agony of wearing a yucky brown coconut suit! We sang, "We are the feast, so feast your eyes. What doesn't rest on your hips will thicken your thighs."

It was Tamika's turn to enter. She sang her opening lines on cue. "I am the mighty coconut. Taste my juice, it's sweet. Crack me open, cook me, I make a tasty treat." She sang confidently as her arms, barely sticking out of her giant coconut suit, kept time to the music.

Cinnamon entered, swirling across the stage in a pig costume. She twirled in a circle, dancing around the fruit, the meat, and the flames.

The audience roared as we stepped forward group by group for the curtain call. As I watched them clapping for us, I felt proud to have been part of the musical even if, technically speaking, I'd only played a small role in making it happen.

ANIMAL, VEGETABLE, OR MINERAL?

Later that evening I sat on my bed wearing my over-sized *Boston Red Sox* T-shirt. I wasn't exactly a big baseball fan but I just loved that particular shade of red! Too bad it clashed with my newly painted turquoise walls.

My mother leaned in the doorway. "I think the party was a hit. There isn't much food leftover, and if the mess they left downstairs is any indication of the fun they had playing the games..."

Dad popped through the doorway, rubbing his chest. "Isn't anybody going to congratulate the world-renowned winner of this evening's highly competitive domino tournament?"

Abuelo sauntered in after him. "You only won because I on your team."

I rolled my eyes. "The only reason *either* of you won was because of the loud *Salsa* music blaring in the background. No one else could concentrate."

Rosa wandered in. "I thought we were going to watch your new commercial, Daisy?"

"Oh yeah." I checked the clock on the wall. "We'd better get moving. It's coming on soon."

Everyone gathered in front of the TV in the family room. My new commercial was scheduled to air during the first half of The Forceful Fighters Reunion Special. About five minutes into the show, the first commercial came on.

Cockadoodle Doo. A bird crowed as the logo of *El Loco Fried Chicken* appeared on the screen. The camera zoomed in for a close-up of a gentleman devouring a plate of mashed potatoes, black beans, plantains, and fried chicken. Abuelo!

He stopped gorging himself for a nanosecond and said, *"I always go crazy at El Loco Fried Chicken."*

We all cracked up as we watched him shoveling food into his mouth, non-stop.

I glanced over at him. "When did you shoot this?"

"My spare time," he said. "But I don't brag before my chickpeas are hatched."

The music faded, and my commercial came on next.

"Introducing," I said, holding up a purple tube, *"Blueberry Blast! A brand new blueberry-flavored toothpaste that tastes delicious and works great!"* I licked my teeth.

"Yummmmm! Whenever I use delicious-tasting Blueberry Blast, I just have to smile."

After I spoke with Becky Kelsey on the phone, she had decided to change the flavor of *Brocco-Brush* and asked me if I'd try the new version. I did and loved it. Fortunately, everyone else did, too. Finally! My face on a national TV commercial!

I was excited but nervous at the same time. On Monday morning, I'd find out who made the master class. Before then, Tamika and I had some catching up to do.

The next day Dad drove us to the homeless shelter. Dad had quite a bit of leftover paint so we decided to use it to paint some of the rooms in the private area of the shelter. Nathan and Suzanna were joining us and so were a few kids from school like Emma, Ashton, and Enrique, along with their families.

Tamika and I both loved turquoise, so we decided to help paint one of the women's bedrooms that color. We spent most of the morning painting and when we were invited to stay for lunch, without having to help make it, nobody turned down the offer.

On the way to the kitchen, we ran into Brad and Zach in the hallway painting a mural of a nature scene. Tamika and I stopped to dab a few dots of paint onto some butterfly wings. That was about all I could do: paint in the lines. But Brad didn't seem to mind since it was less work for him. I glanced around at the fresh paint everywhere. It didn't just feel good to see the results of all our hard work. It felt good to be friends with Tamika again, too.

Later that day we headed off to the mall and then went to the theater to watch a movie together, just like old times.

———

I ASKED MY DAD IF HE COULD DROP ME OFF AT SCHOOL EARLY ON Monday morning. The professor had said he'd post the list of those who made the master class once the musical was over, and we'd even get to meet some of the teachers since the master class would start soon. I remembered the last time I'd scanned the list when we'd auditioned for the musical. I was hoping it wouldn't be a repeat of what had happened before.

I didn't walk to the list, I ran to it.

When I read it, I couldn't believe my eyes. There at the top of the list was my name, Daisy De La Cruz. I busted out crying right then and there, and I didn't care who saw. I also said a silent prayer of thanks. God had been truly good to me. Just three months earlier I hadn't even shot my first commercial, but since Professor Magoon had shown up in August, I'd gotten more performing experience than I'd had my whole life.

My eyes were blurry as I tried reading the rest of the names. Enrique Alvarado, Manuel Melendez, Ashton (also known as Goldilocks) Ford, Bradley Robinson, Tamika Robinson...

Brad and Tamika had made it, too!

Right then Tamika ran up and saw her name. We held hands and jumped around giggling, screaming, and crying all at the same time.

Cinnamon sauntered up. We hadn't scanned the rest of the list, but I couldn't imagine it not having her name on it. She read the list, gave us her queenly nod and left.

Did she make it or not?

Tamika and I rushed back to the list. We didn't see her name right away, but there it was. Right at the bottom, listed last.

Most people headed back to homeroom after they read the list, but I had to stop by and thank the professor, even if we did have music later that day. I didn't want to wait.

I was about to knock on his door, but drew my hand back when I noticed another man in the office, someone I'd never seen before.

It was too late to leave. The professor had seen me. "Good morning, Miss De La Cruz. I'm actually glad you stopped by. I'd like you to meet an old acquaintance."

The tall man wore a navy pinstriped suit. He strolled over and shook my hand. "I'm Alistaire Hobby, General Manager of the Boca Raton Musical Theatre. The professor here has been telling me a lot about you."

"He has?" *I hope he's been saying good stuff about me.*

"He thought you'd be perfect for a role in one of my children's musicals."

My legs felt like overcooked linguine. *You have to be a serious performer to sing in a real, live, professional musical. I can't believe the professor recommended me.*

Professor Magoon interrupted before I could respond.

"Please don't feel any pressure to agree," the professor told me. "Even though I did drag old Ali down here to help work with our master class, I told him you were one of the hardest working young ladies I'd ever met. Our Daisy here is a real gem, not a diva," he said, winking. "Miss Robinson filled me in on how much you helped her during the show."

Way to go, Tamika!

"We should discuss this with your parents first, of course," added Mr. Hobby.

"Oh...uh...wow," I stammered. "I just have one question." I remembered my doggy suit and chicken getup. "Will I, uh, have to play the part of an animal, vegetable, or mineral?" I squinted my eyes waiting for the answer.

"Well...I...uh..." Now it was Mr. Hobby's turn to stammer. "The role I had in mind is that of a singing cat." He glanced from the professor to me. "But...if you're allergic to cats, I also need to fill the role of a cow and a hippo."

Professor Magoon bit his lip, as if trying to stifle a laugh.

"Oh...no," I finally answered. "I love cats." *Didn't Brad say they taste like bologna? Who doesn't like bologna?* "I've had lots of experience wearing all sorts of costumes. So...no...I mean...yes... I'll look forward to it...thanks."

Mr. Hobby twirled his mustache. "I think we've found ourselves a winner, old chum."

The professor slapped his friend on the back and let out his laugh. "Yes, indeed. I think we have."

Well...a singing cat, or cow, or hippo is still a part in a professional show. I'll be performing the role of Maria Von Trapp soon enough. At least I'll be part of a musical! A real, live, professional musical!

I headed out the door with visions of myself on stage, conducted by Mr. Hobby, living the privileged life, eating ice cream for every meal. I'd have a tutor, a personal hairdresser, a personal make-up artist, a personal assistant, a personal trainer—

"Ah, one more thing, Miss De La Cruz." The professor leaned out of the music room doorway.

I wonder what sort of special gig he's got for me now.

He beamed. "Would you mind lending a hand with the scenery at recess, perhaps? The crew could use some extra help putting things away."

"Of course," I said to the professor. *Oops-a-Daisy!* I said to myself. *But I can still dream, can't I?*

SPANISH WORDS AND PHRASES

Abuelo - grandfather

Adíos - goodbye

Besito – little kiss

Bomba – traditional Puerto Rican dance with drum accompaniment

Bueno – good

Buenas noches – good night

Chiquita – tiny

¿Como está? – How are you?

Dinero – money

El loco – the crazy one

Flan – a custard-like dessert

Hola – hello

La Isla del Encanto – The Island of Enchantment

Mija – my daughter

Mira que loco – how crazy

Monito – little monkey

Nena – child

Papi – dad

Papasito – little daddy

Puerquito – little pig

¿Qué? – What?

¿Qué pasa? – What's happening?

¿Qué pasa ahora? – What's wrong now?

¿Qué voy a hacer? –What should I do?

Rellenos – deep fried mashed potato balls stuffed with seasoned ground beef or pork

Sí - yes

Tostones – savory, crunchy fried plantains

Yo soy – I am

ABOUT THE AUTHOR

Melody Delgado is a classically trained vocalist and has performed in concerts, recitals and conferences along the east coast and overseas. She was also a music educator for a number of years in both Florida and Massachusetts.

Her first job after college was working for an NBC-TV affiliate where she did voiceovers and also shot a commercial where she played the role of a clown. She squeezed a squeaky toy bugle as she sashayed in front of the camera.

Melody has also led and served in benevolent ministries in North America and the Middle East. She currently works as a writer. Look for more books about Daisy and her quirky family in upcoming books included in the series, The De La Cruz Diaries. She has also written ROYALLY ENTITLED, an inspirational, historical romance for women and teens, part of the Brides of Brevalia Series, also published by Clean Reads. You can find her on Facebook, Twitter and at her website.

Melody lives in Florida with her husband and children.

www.melodydelgado.com/

CPSIA information can be obtained
at www.ICGtesting.com
Printed in the USA
FFOW03n1208081017
40766FF